"I've started having dreams about you," Tawny admitted. "About us."

"What kind of dreams?" Simon watched the candlelight flicker over her features.

"Sexual dreams. *Explicit* sexual dreams," she said, shifting restlessly on the sofa.

Heat surged through him, and Simon fought to keep his voice neutral. "They're just dreams, Tawny. Why would you let a few dreams interfere with a real relationship between you and your fiancé?"

"Because I'm having them every night. It's gotten to the point that being asleep is the best part of my day. And I've been feeling guilty as hell, because the sex I have in my dreams is so much better than what Elliott and I have in reality."

Her words seduced him, fired along his nerve endings, tightened his body as if she'd actually trailed her hands over him.

Tawny slowly moved closer to him. "Do you know the first thing that came to mind when I heard you were coming over this evening?" The touch of her fingers on his arm nearly burned him. "I thought maybe we could exorcise those dreams." She drew in a deep breath. "Because as it stands now, Simon, I'm afraid you've ruined me for any other man."

Dear Reader,

The idea for this story came from the movie *Love Actually*—in the subplot of which one character is in love with his best friend's woman. Of course, be it the blessing or bane of a writer, while I loved the premise, I was driven to put my own spin on it. I was burning to write this story, especially since the characters had already taken up residence in my head. So I was thrilled when my editor approved the idea.

Things got *very* interesting when we slotted it for the 24-HOURS: BLACKOUT series. Hmmm. Take one besotted best friend (Simon), one unfaithful fiancé (Elliott) and one woman at the center of it all (Tawny), set the entire book within a twenty-four-hour time frame and plunge New York into a blackout, trapping the hero and heroine in her apartment. Together. In the dark. On a hot summer night. To say it was a challenging story to write is an understatement, but it was also great fun.

I hope you enjoy Simon and Tawny's journey to discovering their own happy ending, one that gets better *after* midnight. I'd love to hear about *your* blackout story. Drop by and visit me at www.jenniferlabrecque.com, or snail mail me at P.O. Box 298, Hiram, GA 30141.

Enjoy the heat....

Jennifer LaBrecque

Books by Jennifer LaBrecque

HARLEQUIN TEMPTATION

DARING IN THE DARK
Jennifer LaBrecque

HARLEQUIN®

TORONTO • NEW YORK • LONDON
AMSTERDAM • PARIS • SYDNEY • HAMBURG
STOCKHOLM • ATHENS • TOKYO • MILAN • MADRID
PRAGUE • WARSAW • BUDAPEST • AUCKLAND

To Rita Herron, Susan Kimoto and Rhonda Nelson
for all the times ya'll have talked me off the ledge
and through the story.

Acknowledgment:
Thanks to John Wehr and his photojournaling of the
2003 NYC blackout at www.johnwehr.com/blackout.

ISBN 0-373-79210-7

DARING IN THE DARK

1

HER HEAD DROPPED TO HIS shoulder, but still she watched the mirror. She knew not to look away. Every time she stopped looking, he stopped touching...and his touch drove her crazy. And yes, watching in the mirror made it so much more intense, so much hotter. His fathomless eyes met hers in the reflection. Her, on his lap, her back against his chest, her legs spread. He reached between her thighs and his long fingers parted her, opening her to his touch and his pleasure. His fingers were dark against her bare, pink flesh, sliding into her yawning, hungry portal...oh, yes...felt so good...please don't stop...watching...wanting...oh, almost there....

The shrill ring of the bedside phone shattered the moment, pulling her out of the dream. Her body tight, her thighs wet, Tawny groped for the phone. "Hello."

"Were you napping?" Elliott said, his normally cheery voice sounding just a bit forced. Of course, she could just be transferring the tension that lingered from being poised on the brink of orgasm in her dream. Or it could be Elliott criticizing her, which seemed to happen more and more frequently. It was almost like spending time with her parents.

"Hmm." As an event planner for a group of Midtown attorneys, her hours weren't nine to five, Monday through Friday. "Last night was the cocktail party for that German client, remember? Then the partners had a lovely working breakfast at six-thirty this morning. Just what I wanted to do, crawl out of bed at four-thirty on a Saturday. Anyway, there's no sin in an afternoon nap." Intense sexual arousal and guilt lent her voice a husky note. "Did you work very late last night?" Elliott invested incredible hours in his art gallery, but it was paying off with a growing reputation and clientele.

"Late enough." He sounded uncharacteristically terse.

Maybe it really was just her. She was wound so tight and ached so badly she wanted to cry. Or come. She should laugh, confess to her husband-to-be that she'd just been having the most awesome dream sex and that she still desperately needed to come and ask him to help her out.

Once upon a time she would've thought laid-back, easygoing Elliott would get off on a round of afternoon phone sex and talking her into an orgasm. But she wasn't so sure anymore. Lately he'd been neither laid-back nor easygoing. And what if somewhere along the way she revealed he wasn't the man spreading her thighs and leading her to ecstasy in her dreams? And what if the man she'd agreed to marry "till death they did part" couldn't pick up where the dream left off and get her to that magical place?

He continued and the opportunity was gone. "I thought I'd come over after the gallery closes this evening."

"That's fine as long as you bring dinner and we stay in." If he called this late in the day, she sure wasn't cooking. Elliott was more into clubbing and being seen than she was. A quiet night at home suited her.

"Staying in works. I wanted to talk to you."

Tawny propped up on her pillow. She and Elliott talked often, but when someone announced they *wanted* to talk… "What?"

"It's too complicated to go into over the phone."

"That's a lousy thing to do. Bring it up and leave me hanging."

"Sorry. But let's leave it till tonight." It wasn't her imagination. He definitely sounded strained.

"Okay…" Sex. It must be about sex. Of course at this point her brain *was* one-tracking.

"Thai sound okay?"

"Sure. You know what I like." Elliott couldn't possibly miss her flirtatious innuendo. Maybe he'd initiate a little phone sex without her asking.

Elliott cleared his throat, as if her teasing left him uncomfortable. "Um, yeah, I'll pick up chicken curry."

Nix the phone sex. "Chicken curry sounds good."

He cleared his throat again. He was either nervous or coming down with something. "I thought I'd bring Simon along."

Her hand tightened on the phone even as her internal temperature slid up the sizzle scale. "Simon?" She licked her suddenly dry lips and rolled over onto her belly. "Why would he want to come to my apartment? He's avoided me like the plague ever since the photo shoot. He obviously dislikes me."

"He's a busy guy. I don't think he dislikes you. Simon's just…"

"Dark. Brooding. Cynical. Intense. I think that about covers it." And sexy in a shiver-down-her-spine, her-head-needed-to-be-examined kind of way. But that didn't seem the most prudent observation to make about her fiancé's best friend.

Elliott laughed and Tawny was thankful it didn't bother him that she obviously rubbed Simon the wrong way. Sometimes she wondered if Elliott didn't prefer it that way, but she'd dismissed the notion as unworthy of Elliott.

"Simon's just Simon," he said. "Can he come, too?"

Could he come? She grew wetter still, her whole body flushing and her nipples pebbling harder. Intense, brooding Simon, with his faint British accent, had been the one in her dream.

"Tawny?" Elliott prompted on the other end of the line.

She squirmed on the hard mattress. "No. I don't

mind if he comes." Simply saying it aroused her even more. Guilt and shame fed the dark lust Simon inspired in her on a nearly nightly basis. Now it was getting even worse—she'd only taken an afternoon nap. He was her fiancé's best friend, he despised her and every night he was the source of soul-shattering sex in her dreams.

"We'll see you a little after nine then."

She hung up and closed her eyes. Why was Simon coming with Elliott? Why the three of them? What would they do?

With her body strung tight and humming with arousal, a dark fantasy bloomed in her. The three of them, here in her bedroom. Elliott, golden haired and fair, Simon, dark. Two sexy men intent on touching and tasting every inch of her, all with the singular purpose of pleasuring her.

She blinked her eyes open and reached into the drawer of her bedside table, pulling out her vibrator. She couldn't go through the afternoon this way.

Elliott was her fiancé. He was funny and generous and warm, most of the time. She might not have control of her dreams, but she was wide-awake now.

Despite her best efforts to focus on Elliott, it was Simon she came for as she shuddered her way to an orgasm.

"YOU LOOK LIKE HELL," SIMON Thackeray said as he carefully placed his camera case in an orange vinyl chair in Elliott's inner sanctum and sat in the matching chair.

Blond, good-looking, outgoing and possessing a sense of style that always left him looking as if he'd just stepped off the pages of *GQ*, Elliott turned heads in a crowd. A girl in college had once likened the two best friends to Apollo and Hades. They were foils in both looks and personality. Elliott, sunny and outgoing, Simon, dark, quiet, withdrawn. But Elliott had sounded weary and worried on the phone when he'd asked Simon to stop by. He didn't look any better than he'd sounded. "What's going on?"

Elliott perched on the edge of the stainless-steel desk and swung one leg. "We've been friends a long time."

Simon nodded at the obvious. Since they'd met in a photography class in junior high, where they'd discovered a shared love of art and a friendship that had weathered the years. Elliott had thrown out a lifeline that saved Simon from drowning in his own loneliness. Conversely Simon had anchored Elliott, provided him with some much-needed stability. Elliott's parents were warm and outgoing, but volatile.

He wasn't so sure he would've pursued a career in photography if Elliott hadn't believed in him and pushed him. And Simon had provided invaluable contacts when Elliott had decided to open a small gallery.

"You know you're the brother I never had," Elliott

continued. "I've always thought I could tell you anything. Share anything." Once upon a time Simon had felt the same way. Until he'd discovered that there were some things you couldn't share with your best friend. Like being in love with his fiancée. "I hope you'll always be my friend."

Simon sighed at Elliott's penchant for melodrama. If Elliott hadn't parlayed his art-history degree and eye for art into owning a gallery, he could've given Broadway a run. "Elliott, unless you've ax-murdered a little old lady, I'm going to always be your friend." Simon shrugged. "I'd probably be your friend even then. Why don't you just tell me what this is all about?"

"I'm gay."

"Right."

First Elliott called him in and gave him the big friendship spiel, now we was fooling around when Simon had a photo shoot scheduled in forty-five minutes. Elliott had a warped sense of humor and a piss-poor sense of timing.

Elliott knotted his hands together. "This isn't a joke. I'm serious. I'm gay."

Simon sat, stunned. Elliott was…gay? How was that possible? They'd been best friends for over a decade. Simon was the odd straight guy in a profession that attracted homosexuals like a homing device, yet he'd never once suspected Elliott of anything but blatant heterosexuality.

For God's sake, Elliott was engaged to Tawny, slept with her on a regular basis and he'd just announced he was gay? "When…how…"

"Perhaps *bisexual* is a better estimation." Elliott ran his manicured hand through his short blond hair. "I've found myself increasingly attracted to men over the last several years." He shook his head and offered a harsh laugh lacking in humor. "Don't worry. Not you."

Quite frankly Simon could give a toss if Elliott was attracted to him or not. Well…maybe he was a bit relieved Elliott hadn't professed undying love or lust for him, but he'd definitely missed something along the way.

Simon clearly recalled the first time he'd seen Tawny. It'd been here in the gallery, outside Elliott's office. Simon had dropped by during a private event—a cocktail party and private viewing Tawny had arranged for her company. She'd been engrossed in an animated discussion with the caterer. One look at her and his world had shifted into sharper focus. Then she'd disappeared and he'd sought out Elliott, intent on discovering who she was, only to learn Elliott had beat him to the punch. Before Simon had opened his mouth, Elliott had announced he'd met his dream woman and arranged a date with her. Intuitively Simon had known it was the same woman. And he'd been right.

"What was this six months ago when you told me you'd just met the woman of your dreams?" he asked.

"She was hot and sexy and so different from the other women in New York, I thought she might *cure* me."

She'd been a bloody cure?

Simon pushed to his feet and walked over to the window overlooking the street, needing to look at something other than the friend he wasn't sure he knew any longer. Elliott had always been a bit self-absorbed, but this....

Outside, Manhattanites shared the sidewalk with tourists. Customers thronged from the electronics store across the street to the corner falafel stand and the shops in between. A cabbie flipped off a delivery van who cut him off.

Like a strip of negatives laid out before him, he saw in his head photos, moments in time committed to memory. He'd wagered the more he was around Tawny, the more he knew of her, the more his attraction would diminish. Instead with every encounter he'd found himself increasingly drawn to her, discovering that her spirit, her wit, her spunk, ran even deeper and surer than her physical beauty.

And he'd held himself increasingly aloof. Afraid he'd betray himself with a careless glance, a misplaced remark, he hid behind sardonic comments. He'd still held out hope for himself, for a recovery, even after Elliott proposed. He'd get over her.

It had been the photo shoot, the day he'd spent photographing Tawny, at Elliott's request, that he knew he was deeply, irrevocably in love with her. He gripped the windowsill and rocked on the balls of his feet, looking inward instead of at the busy street outside. It was the only time he'd ever spent alone with her and he'd glimpsed something so sweet, so elusive, that to end that day had bordered on physical pain.

And she'd been a bloody cure for Elliott. He turned around to face Elliott, struggling for an even tone. "And was asking her to marry you part of the cure or did you consider yourself cured at that juncture? I'm a bit confused. Is this a twelve-step program?"

"Does it make you feel good to be such a sarcastic bastard?"

"Not particularly." Simon felt a foreign urge to pound Elliott's head against the cinnamon-colored wall. "You asked her to marry you when you knew you felt this way? When you knew you were attracted to men?"

Elliott colored at Simon's censure. "But I'm also attracted to her. I thought if I threw myself into the relationship enough these feelings would go away." He stood and shoved his hands into his pockets. He began to pace the room.

"But they didn't and you cheated on Tawny?"

Elliott squared his shoulders defensively. "Just once. Last night. You know Richard, the acrylics painter we're featuring? I've caught him looking at me, watching me a couple of times. Anyway, we were working late last night, shared a bottle of wine and one thing led to another."

Perhaps this was one big mistake Elliott was blowing out of proportion through guilt. Elliott was also a bit of a dramatist, and guilt distorted the clearest picture, as Simon well knew. "Did you have too much wine? Were you drunk?"

His blue eyes solemn, Elliott shook his head. "No. That'd be an easy excuse. I wasn't drunk. I was intrigued. I thought I'd try it and know for sure, one way or the other." He scrubbed his hand over his forehead. "I liked it. I have feelings for Richard."

Simon squelched a frown of distaste. This shouldn't be any different than listening to Elliott talk about a woman. But it was. Vastly different. Simon held up a staying hand. "I neither want nor need details."

"I wasn't offering them. That was merely by way of clarification," Elliott said, clearly put out. "I've got to tell Tawny. She deserves to know."

"Bloody right she deserves to know." The risks associated with homosexuality slammed him in the gut. Concern for both Tawny and Elliott sharpened his tone. "I hope you used a rubber."

"Of course I did." Elliott slumped into a chair and dropped his head onto the back. "That's just one of the reasons I need to tell her. If we stay together—" that knife twisted in Simon's gut "—she has to make an informed decision."

"You like sex with Richard but you're going to sleep with Tawny?" Simon said.

Elliott creased a sheet of paper between his fingers. "I love her. What's not to love? She's sexy, smart, warm and generous. But we're not setting off any fireworks in the bedroom. I'm attracted to her, but it's not as exciting as it is with Richard."

Elliott had just handed him far more information on several fronts than he'd ever wanted. And he was driving Simon mad, fidgeting with that piece of paper. "Would you put the paper down?" Elliott shot him a look but tossed it onto the desk. "So you don't want to break off the engagement?" Simon asked, his head beginning to throb from tension.

"I don't know. She's a great woman. I need some time to think. I guess whether we break off the engagement is up to her." He ran his hand over the back of his neck. "This is going to be a hell of a conversation." Elliott drew a deep breath and whooshed it out. "Come with me to tell her."

"No." This was between Elliott and Tawny. And talk about a conflict of interest. Simon wanted her, but not with a broken heart or as a rebound lover. However, she *would* be available if this went down the way he thought it would.

Elliott braced his hands on the desk and leaned toward Simon. "Please. I need you for moral support. This is going to be one of the hardest things I've ever done."

Elliott hated facing unpleasant tasks alone. From the time they'd met and become fast friends, he'd dragged Simon along to face teachers, professors, his parents. He'd always maintained Simon was stronger than he was. But for once Simon wasn't being dragged into Elliott's mess. This time his friend was flying solo.

He shook his head. "It's private, Elliott."

"You were there when I proposed," Elliott argued.

Simon crossed his arms over his chest. "And if I had known you were going to propose, I wouldn't have been." Outgoing, give-me-an-audience Elliott had chosen a double date to propose. Simon recalled the agony that had ripped through him when Elliott had presented Tawny with a yellow-diamond engagement ring over dessert. Simon's date, Lenore, had thought it quite romantic.

"This is a mess. I need you there when I tell her. I called her and asked to come over tonight after the gallery closes." He stopped pacing and faced Simon, the length of the room separating them. "I told her you were coming, too."

Simon squashed the adolescent urge to ask Elliott what she'd said about him coming round. He and Elliott had always supported each other. They'd always watched one another's back. But he wasn't sure if he could bear to see the hurt and betrayal on Tawny's face. Nor did he have the right to witness that. "You shouldn't have done that."

"Please, Simon."

But he hadn't exactly been coming through for Elliott all the nights Simon had lain in his lonely bed and made love to Tawny in his head. His conscience smote him. He had no business going. He didn't want to go. But he owed Elliott, whether Elliott knew it or not, for every licentious thought he'd ever had about Tawny. For all the times and all the ways he'd had her in his head.

Guilt did crazy things to men—left them agreeing to things they would otherwise run away from.

"Okay, I'll go. But I'll have to meet you there," Simon said. He stood and picked up his equipment bag.

Elliott dropped into his chair, his relief evident. "Nine o'clock. Her place. Do you remember the way?"

He'd dropped her off once with Elliott. "Sure." He shifted the camera bag to his shoulder and turned for the door.

"Simon…" Elliott said.

He turned again to face Elliott.

"You're a good friend."

Righto. He was a good friend to be obsessively, compulsively in love with his best friend's woman.

2

TAWNY GLANCED AT THE CLOCK on her dresser. Fifteen minutes until Elliott and Simon arrived. She discarded her skirt on the closet floor and defiantly pulled on a pair of shorts. She'd gotten home from running errands and had plenty of time to shower and shave her legs. And now she was dithering about what to wear. As if it mattered.

Her fiancé and his best friend, the guy who disliked her intensely, were coming over with take-out Thai. After a year of living here, one of the things she still loved about New York was the variety of fabulous food within blocks, even if a Southern-girl transplant couldn't find grits or sweet tea.

She looked over the clothes in her closet. It wasn't as if they were going anywhere or she was looking to impress anyone. She picked up a faded T-shirt from her very first 5K run and promptly discarded it. Nah, Elliott had a thing about her dressing up, even if they were staying in. And even though she wasn't entering a beauty contest, her Southern upbringing drew the line at having anyone over and wearing *that*.

She laughed at herself. And no, she still couldn't bring herself to wear white after Labor Day or before Easter. She might be living on Manhattan's Upper West Side but she'd always be Tawny Edwards with Savannah, Georgia, sensibilities. Funny, she'd come to New York to find out who she was and what she was about. She smiled. Wouldn't her mother be surprised that the rebellious Edwards family screw-up still adhered to the rules of white?

She settled instead on a halter wrap. Casual but sexy. And more important, cool—a major plus considering how stinking hot it was outside. She finished dressing and closed the closet door on the discarded clothes littering the floor. She pulled her hair up and clipped it haphazardly with a giant barrette underneath. Even with the air-conditioning cranked, the sweltering heat seemed to seep inside.

She spritzed perfume behind her ears and, on a defiant whim, sprayed it between her breasts. Simon might not like her, but dammit, he'd at least like the way she smelled.

She sang along with a Roberta Flack remake playing on the radio in the other room. She loved the evening program—Sensual Songs and Decadent Dedications—which offered a nice mix of old and new love songs. And who cared if she was off-key?

She tugged at her shorts. She'd skipped her run this morning and she felt it in their snug fit. Some women were blessed with svelte, slender bodies that actually fit into sylphlike fashions. She, however, didn't belong to that club. She'd learned long ago that eating half of what was on her plate and exercising every day was the only thing that kept her from resembling the Pillsbury Doughboy in drag. Petite and curvy all too easily slid into short and fat.

Tawny made the mistake of double-checking her behind in the mirror while she sang about him killing her softly with his song. Ugh. It was still there…all of it and then some. Elliott was right. The last time they were in bed, he'd mentioned that her butt had gotten bigger. Not exactly what she'd wanted to hear, but she supposed the truth sometimes hurt.

She'd seriously considered having her ass liposuctioned with her last bonus, but what if those fat cells relocated to her thighs or some other equally heinous body destination? Unwilling to risk fat-cell transference, she did an extra set of butt-killing donkey lifts every other day. And from the looks of things, it was time to make that a daily habit.

An outraged yowl in the other room diverted her attention from the shortcomings—or rather the over-abundance—of her behind. She went into the kitchen and dumped a measure of cat food into the empty bowl by the refrigerator.

"Uh-huh. You're as close to wasting away as I am." She laughed and snatched Peaches up for a quick hug before he squirmed out of her arms. "But I understand. I'm hungry, too." She put him down in front of his food bowl.

Peaches, a five-year-old declawed Maine coon abandoned by his former owner and promptly rescued from the animal shelter on his last day before the big E—as in euthanasia—in no way resembled a peach in either coloring, countenance, or personality. However, Tawny had named him that because it reminded her of her Georgia roots without bringing home too close. Which probably made no sense to the rest of the world but perfect sense to Tawny.

One might reckon that Peaches would be grateful to have been snatched from the jaws of certain death and appropriately fawn over his savior. One would be wrong. It had been Peaches's arrogance in the face of his impending demise that had stolen Tawny's heart and sealed the feline's fate.

The sound of the buzzer reverberated through the apartment and Tawny's heart thudded in her chest. Simon and Elliott. The idea of coming face-to-face with Simon had tormented her all afternoon. She hadn't seen him since he'd begun to invade her dreams, and subsequently her body, in a most satisfying, but totally disquieting, manner.

She swallowed and turned the radio down on her way to the door. Peering through the peephole, her heart hammered even harder as Simon's lean face stared—not at the door but down the hall, as if he'd actually prefer to be anywhere rather than outside her apartment.

On the radio Etta James crooned in a low, sultry voice, about her love coming along at last and the end of her lonely days, which did nothing to dispel Tawny's nervousness and the sexual anticipation curling through her.

She mentally slapped herself around. Get a grip. So in her dreams she'd had wild monkey sex with Simon. By no stretch of her overactive, oversexed imagination was *he* her own true love coming along.

She squared her shoulders, pasted on her best loaded-with-Southern-charm smile, slipped the locks and opened her door. "Hi, Simon."

"Hullo, Tawny." It was wickedly unfair the way his voice, with its hint of British accent, revved her engine. That was one thing about her dreams—he always talked to her during sex and it always turned her on. This was no dream, but she'd been conditioned and felt a familiar heat stir within her.

She looked past him. "Where's Elliott?"

"I had a shoot today so we came separately," he said without a glimmer of a smile in the depth of his dark eyes.

Tawny stepped aside. "Come in."

His dark hair, cut close and combed back, lent his lean face an ascetic look. She felt his body heat as he stepped past her into the room, his camera equipment slung over his shoulder. This was much worse than she'd anticipated, far more potent than any dream. His clean, subtle scent teased her. In her dreams his scent didn't entice her as it did now. She caught her breath and strove for a light tone.

"How was your photo shoot?"

"Fine. It went quick. I've shot Chloe before," Simon said.

The name evoked an image of a tall, thin, beautiful model. Tawny didn't feel the slightest twinge of remorse at hating the unknown, unsuspecting Chloe—that was the price paid by thin, beautiful women without an ass the size of a principality.

A few weeks ago, after their engagement, Simon had photographed Tawny at Elliott's request. Elliott possessed an eye for art, but he wasn't an artist. Simon, however, was a genius with a camera. She wasn't a professional model and it had taken an entire day of Simon working with her, cajoling her, but her photographs had been fantastic. She'd seen herself in a different way. She'd seen strength, but also a sensual vulnerability.

He'd been patient and almost charming, as if when he got behind the camera he forgot himself or perhaps he could truly be himself.

During the shoot, she'd thought she'd finally reached Elliott's best friend, won him over. It had been a magical day. But then afterward he'd retreated even further behind a wall, cooler and more aloof than ever. Mercifully their paths hadn't crossed since.

Except at night. In her bed. In her dreams. The night following the photo shoot she'd dreamed of erotic, explicit sex with Simon. And every night since. Now the object of her writhing lust stood in her apartment, having spent the day photographing some skinny model. Tawny bit back a bitchy comment.

"I haven't seen you to tell you I thought the photos you took of me were great. Not that I'm great, but the photos were. You're very good at what you do." Whoa. Instant image of him bringing her to orgasm in her dream. "I mean, you're good with your camera." She closed the door. *Tawny, honey, find a brain cell and grab on to it.* She sounded like a dithering idiot.

"You're very photogenic. You have a great smile and good bone structure," he said.

He spoke very matter-of-factly. He could've been discussing the weather. There was absolutely no reason for her heart to pound as if he'd just claimed her beauty equal to that of the legendary Helen of Troy. She felt as gauche as she had when she'd been a third-grader and Henry Turner had pulled her braids. Except she'd liked Henry Turner. And while she might have toe-curling dreams about Simon, she wasn't altogether sure that she liked him.

"Thank you. Your equipment should be safe here." She indicated a spot between the door and the antique cupboard to the right. Hauling *that* monstrosity up when she'd moved last year had been a party. "Would you like a drink while we're waiting on Elliott? Red wine?"

Simon placed his camera and equipment on the floor next to the cupboard with more care and consideration than many mothers with babies. He glanced at her over his shoulder. "Absolutely."

Earth to Tawny. She should stop admiring the way his black T-shirt hugged his shoulders and the lean line of his back. She should also stop eyeing the fit of his jeans over his very fine—make that *extra* fine—ass.

He stood, pivoting to face her in one fluid movement. He arched a questioning brow. "Need any help?"

Don't mind me. I was just checking out your eye candy. "No. Going right now." She indicated the sofa with a flick of her wrist. "Make yourself at home. I'll be right back."

She fled the room, silently urging Elliott to arrive soon. Those dreams were seriously messing with her head. She'd felt as if his gaze, hot and consuming, had licked across her shoulders bared by her halter top and across her buttocks snugged into her shorts.

She leaned against the counter and dragged in a calming breath, dismissing her ridiculous notions. Simon had been his usual remote self since he'd arrived. The only heat she'd felt from him had been a product of her own twisted, overactive, inappropriate imagination.

She reached past Peaches to the small wine rack

atop the fridge and pulled out a bottle of cabernet. Peaches, who spent most of his time on top of the refrigerator, offered her a lazy slit-eyed look.

Tawny uncorked the bottle. "You know, normal cats curl up on a bed or in the corner of the sofa or drape themselves across a chair back. Why do you camp out on top of the refrigerator?"

Of course, the cat didn't deign to answer. Tawny pulled three wineglasses out of the cabinet. She personally thought Peaches liked to render himself inaccessible. And what did it say about her that she loved that damn cat? "Don't mind me. I'm leaving now."

She went back into the den.

Simon sat on her purple chenille sofa studying the room. Self-consciousness surged through her, knowing he was seeing her personal space through the eyes of an artist. Her taste tended toward eclectic. She favored reproduction art, the occasional antique and furniture more comfortable than stylish.

She placed the wine and glasses on the bamboo chest that doubled as a coffee table. Simon focused his attention on her, and she wished contrarily that he was eying her apartment once again instead. The glow from a stained-glass floor lamp at the corner of the sofa backlit him. Dark hair, dark slashing eyebrows above dark eyes, unsmiling visage, black T-shirt and jeans. He was a dark angel come to torment her.

His eyes snared her. The room shrank to just the few feet separating them. If this was one of her dreams, she'd join him on the couch, where she'd nibble and lick her way past his perpetual reserve until they were both getting naked....

"Do you need any help?" he asked.

"Thanks, I've got it." *Don't mind me while I stand here like some whacked-out nympho and fantasize about taking your clothes off while we wait on Elliott to show up.* She disgusted herself. "Glass of wine coming right up."

She managed to pour two glasses. She handed him one, taking care not to touch him in the exchange.

"Were you talking to someone in the kitchen?" he asked. Surely that wasn't amusement lurking in the austere Simon's eyes.

She sat in the armchair on her side of the coffee table, the farthermost point away from him in the confines of her tiny den. Avoiding even the most casual physical contact seemed a good plan. "My cat."

"And does it talk back?"

Whaddaya know? Simon actually owned a sense of humor. "No. He's a typical male. Selective hearing. He only talks if it concerns his empty belly. Or the remote."

"My kind of cat." Simon's spontaneous grin did crazy things to her insides. He silently held his glass up in a toast and then sipped.

His fingers, long and lean, wrapped around the glass stem and reminded her of her afternoon dream and where his fingers had been then.

Simply thinking about it left her wet and wanton again. Great. She'd sit here across from him, drinking wine, waiting on her future husband to show up, and wind up with a wet spot. *Stop.* She would not sit around fantasizing about this man. It was wrong. Guilt churned in her gut. *Thinking* about Simon turned her on faster and hotter than Elliott's actual touch.

She only had to make it through the evening. A few short hours. And next week she was signing up for therapy. Alison, one of the executive secretaries, saw a therapist weekly. First thing Monday morning she'd ask Alison for a referral. This *thing* for Simon was getting out of hand. God knows what would happen if he'd offered a smidgen of interest or encouragement. What kind of woman ran around in perpetual lust for her fiancé's best friend? And it had actually started her thinking, quite hard, as to exactly how she felt about Elliott and whether marrying him was such a good idea. She and Elliott were good together. They got along well. They had fun. But it was nothing like the dark passion with Simon that haunted her dreams. Toss in a vague sense of discontent with her bedroom time with Elliott….

Did she break it off with someone based on hot dreams about someone else? Which came first? Her discontent with Elliott or this dark sexual attraction to Simon? Was she truly attracted or just scared of commitment? Definitely time for a therapist.

"Good wine. Thanks," Simon said.

"Sure." Nervous, she swigged her wine instead of sipping and promptly choked. Then choked some more. Dammit, she couldn't catch her breath.

Simon skirted the chest and took her wineglass from her. He knelt down and, as if conditioned by her dreams, she automatically spread her legs to accommodate him. He grabbed her shoulders. "Can you breathe? Nod your head."

She nodded yes. But he didn't take his hands from her bare skin. Finally the choking fit ended. She was left with him kneeling between her thighs, his fingers curled around the curves of her shoulders, her face hot with humiliation, her body hotter still at his proximity.

"I'm…fine," she said, her voice wavering. Not from her choking spell but from his touch, the brush of his body against her bare legs. The reality of his touch was a thousand times more potent than a mere dream. Did his hand tremble against her shoulder or was it her own reaction?

Simon released her and stood abruptly. Still between her legs, he looked down at her. "You might want to save the chugging for Kool-Aid or beer," he drawled. He turned on his heel and picked up his own wineglass to sit once again on the sofa.

Bite me. Tawny hated him at that moment. How could he be so concerned and considerate one minute and then snide and nasty the next? She ignored his comment and focused instead on Elliott. She glanced at her watch. Almost nine-fifteen.

"Elliott should be here soon. I hope so. I'm starving," she said. Yeah. Simon had just spent the day photographing one of the skin-'n'-bones set and she'd just presented her well-padded ass as starving. "Well, not starving, obviously, but hungry." She simply couldn't say or do anything right in front of him.

And then it didn't matter because she wasn't in front of Simon. She was in utter pitch-black darkness and sudden silence.

"What the hell?" Simon said.

Her sentiments exactly.

"Simon?" Panic filled her voice.

"I'm right here," he said. He stood, blind in the dark. He bumped his shins against the chest. Cautiously he put his wineglass down.

Damn good thing he did because Tawny grabbed onto his arm, startling him, the uncustomary tremor in her voice reflected in her fingers. "I'm sorry. I've got a thing about the dark."

Moving slowly, he felt his way around the furniture until he reached her side. He'd never experienced such absolute darkness. He couldn't see her, but he felt her body heat, smelled her perfume, felt her energy pulsing in her hand on his arm, heard the soft pant of her panic. "A thing?"

"Yeah, I don't like it worth a damn." Her laugh verged on pathetic and tugged at his heartstrings. As if everything she did didn't tug at them. "Curiosity got the better of me and I managed to lock myself in a closet for a couple of hours when I was four. I was terrified. Ever since, the dark freaks me out."

She laughed again, and if he hadn't been so tuned in to the nuances of her voice, he might've missed the nervousness still lurking behind it. Against his better judgment—touching her, as he'd found a few minutes ago, was definitely bad judgment—he caught her hand in his. "It's okay. I'm here. Does your building lose power often?"

"Twice before. But it was always during the day." Her voice sounded surer, less panicked, and her hand was steadier. She tried to pull her hand from his. "I'm fine now."

Her slight breathlessness gave her away. She wasn't fine, but she was doing her best to give that impression. He fought the urge to pull her closer, wrap his arms around her soft vulnerability and reassure her everything was okay. Instead he contented himself with clasping her hand tighter. "Well, I'm not. I'm blind as a bloody bat in here. Where's your flashlight?" he asked.

She turned into him and her cheek brushed against his shoulder, setting his heart racing. It was agony to be so close to her, touch her, smell her.

"I don't have one. It got broken when I moved and I keep forgetting to replace it." Her breath feathered against his neck and her hair teased along his jaw.

"Okay. No flashlight. Move on to plan B. Where's a window?"

Her fingers curled around his. "My bedroom. There's one in the bathroom, but it's small."

"Okay. Lead on to your bedroom." Despite the dark, he closed his eyes when he spoke. Under different circumstances…

"This way." She tugged him by the hand and within seconds he ran into something hard.

"Ow. Damn." Obviously the wall.

"Sorry," she apologized, her disembodied voice beside him.

He rolled his shoulder. "I take it you didn't hit the wall."

"No. I'm in the doorway."

Brilliant. She was laughing at him. Actually banging into walls was rather funny but hard on the shoulder.

"Walking beside you isn't going to work. I'll walk behind you." He braced his hands on her bare shoulders. In the dark he could well imagine her naked. Correction. It was as if she *was* naked, the way he'd imagined her so many times before. Her shoulders were soft, her skin like warm, supple suede. Her scent surrounded him, seduced him. He ached to pull her back into him, to lower his head and kiss the delicate skin at the back of her neck, shower kisses along the curve of her shoulder. He wanted to absorb her heat, her taste, *her.*

Longing pierced his very soul. To have her in his arms but still out of reach was cruel beyond measure. Just one taste of her... He leaned forward and she swayed ever so slightly back into him, tensing beneath his fingertips. Wisps of hair brushed his face. What the hell was he doing? He jerked his head back.

"Simon?" The husky way she said his name always curled heat through him.

"Give me a second to get my bearings." Clothes. He needed to touch clothes. "How about this?" He grasped her full, round hips just below the curve of her waist, the same way he would if they were dancing in a conga line. Yeah, or having sex from behind.

"That's fine." Her voice sounded strained. Or maybe it was just him. This proximity had him near daft.

"Okay. Lead the way." Sod it if he sounded harsh. Better she think him rude than randy.

He walked behind her, keeping a firm grip on her hips, trying to ignore the sweet sway beneath his fingertips. Wouldn't she be impressed? While she fought off a panic attack, he was getting a stiffy from merely touching her and inhaling her scent with every breath he took.

In the room behind them Tawny's cell phone rang. She hesitated, tensing, turning slightly in the direction of the ring. Simon tightened his hold on her. "Just keep going. We don't have a chance of getting to it before it goes to voice mail. Not to mention banging the hell out of us along the way."

They resumed their dark journey. Almost immediately Simon's cell vibrated at his side. "Hold on. Someone's ringing me." He plucked his cell off his side and flipped it open one-handed, keeping the other hand on her hip. "Thackeray here."

"Simon, are you with Tawny?" Elliott asked without preamble.

"Yes. She's right here."

"I just tried to call her and she didn't answer." Elliott's voice held a petulant note.

"It's pitch-black in her apartment. She couldn't get to it in time. Where are you?" Bugger, Elliott. He should be the one here with his hand on Tawny's hip, tortured by the feel of soft flesh and her womanly scent. Except it wouldn't be torture for Elliott because she wasn't off limits to him.

"I'm at the gallery. We don't have any lights either."

"Why are you there? What's going on?"

"I don't think we're under siege, if that's what you mean. I think it's one of those blackouts like we had a couple of years ago. I was running late. Richard and I had a few things to iron out and then everything shut down."

Simon welcomed the dark. Tawny couldn't see the expression on his face. He didn't give a farthing about Richard and Elliott's details, but if Elliott had been here with take-out Thai as arranged, then Simon wouldn't be holding on to Tawny in the dark. Alone. Tempted nearly beyond measure.

"Excellent. How long do you think it'll take you to get here?" Simon asked, deliberately keeping his voice neutral.

"We're locked in. When the electrical system is compromised, the security system goes into total lockdown."

This was getting better and better. "You're locked in at the gallery?"

"That's it in a nutshell." Simon heard the murmur of another man's voice in the background followed by Elliott's breathless laughter. "Listen, you don't have to stay with Tawny. I'm sure she'll be okay."

Hot anger lanced him at Elliott's careless, cavalier regard for Tawny. This afternoon he'd been annoyed with Elliott. Now Simon was furious with his friend. Did he not know or simply not care that the woman who met life head-on was terrified of the dark while he was cozied up with his new lover? What the hell had he been doing hanging out with Richard instead of meeting at Tawny's the way he'd set it up? Where did Elliott get off taking that proprietorial tone when he told Simon he didn't have to stay? And there was no way he could say any of that to Elliott with Tawny listening.

"Of course, I'll stay with her until the power's back on. I wouldn't dream of leaving her alone."

She moved closer to him, and without thinking he tightened his hand on her hip. They'd both shifted during his phone call and now her left hip nudged his,

his hand was still on her other hip, his arm wrapped around the curve of her back. This was bad—very, very bad. How long would he be trapped in this apartment with this woman who drove him crazy? Who touched him somewhere deep inside? Who seemed to slip past every barrier he'd ever erected? His body thought it brilliant, his mind recognized it as a big mistake.

"No. I said you don't need to stay," Elliott snapped.

What the hell? Simon didn't want Tawny to know Elliott was so bloody self-absorbed that he'd have Simon leave her alone in a blackout. Better that his selfish friend appear the considerate fiancé he should be than wound her with the truth. "Don't give it another thought. I won't leave until the electricity's restored."

"Whatever. Go ahead and play Sir Galahad." Elliott, the bastard, actually sounded peevish.

Simon hung up on him and put the phone back on his hip. "That was Elliott. He's fine. He thinks this is a blackout. He's stuck at the gallery with the acrylics painter. In the event of an electrical failure, the security system locks down."

"Apparently Elliott asked you to stay. You don't have to babysit me. I'll be fine."

Piss it all. This was a fine conundrum. He'd never wanted to leave a place more in his life, to flee the hounds of hell nipping at his feet—those beasts of longing and desire that made it nearly unbearable to be in her presence. On the other hand, he didn't think she relished being abandoned during a blackout and he couldn't bring himself to leave her alone. He knew it had been sheer terror and a gut response when she'd clenched his hand earlier but now she didn't want to be an obligation.

"I know I don't have to stay, but I'd rather not have to make my way home without benefit of the subway. Do you mind if I stay until the power's restored?"

"Not at all. I'd like for you to stay if you want to."

He tried to lighten the moment. "Then it's settled. You're stuck with me until then." *Please let it be sooner than later.*

Her laughter sounded more relaxed and he knew he'd done the right thing. "Okay. Looks like we're stuck with one another."

He wasn't sure exactly how it happened, but in that moment…she moved…he moved…in the inky black, and his hand closed over her breast. For several stunned moments he could only stand there, his hand wrapped around her soft breast, her nipple stabbing against his palm through her shirt material.

Like a sudden summer storm, the atmosphere shifted and thickened. A sexual charge pulsed between them. For one daft moment, he could have sworn she leaned into his touch, pushed her pebbled point harder into his hand. Want slammed through him, his universe reduced to the feel of her breast in his palm, the hot desire that left him rigid. She uttered a muted, inarticulate sound. He wasn't sure if it was a moan or a protest, but it served as a dash of cold water.

He yanked his hand away. "I'm sorry. That was an accident."

"Of course it was…I'm sure…you'd never…"

"How far are we from your bedroom?" he asked, his tone as tense as his body.

"Simon…"

She thought he only had to touch her breast and he was ready to throw her down and have his wicked way with her? Ready to fondle her and taste her until she was so caught up in their passion she'd forget all about the dark? Unfortunately she was right. And if she was his, he'd do just that. But she wasn't his. "The window—that's where the window is, isn't it?"

"Yes." Was that relief or embarrassment or both in that single syllable? He left it alone.

They navigated the short hall to her bedroom, past the bed and over to the window. Tawny opened the curtains and raised the blinds.

The city lay shrouded in darkness, reminiscent of a well-rendered charcoal sketch, dark skies with the looming shadows of darker buildings against it. In the distance auxiliary-lit buildings stood, glowing sentinels guarding the city. Up and down the street, candles, flashlights and headlamps provided illumination.

Despite the muffled noise of people and the inevitable bleating of car horns, the darkness isolated them, stranded them on the island of her apartment, removed from the rest of civilization.

Dark clouds scudded across the sky, obliterating the bit of light the night sky might have afforded.

"A storm's coming in," she said.

"It looks like it. Do you have any candles?"

"No flashlight, but I have lots of candles."

She released his hand and turned. Her bedside table stood a few feet from the window. She opened the drawer and felt around. She held up a long object. "My flamethrower."

She flicked a long-nosed, handled lighter and lit a candle by her bed. She crossed the room, lighting two wall sconces. They flanked a painting of a semi-dressed woman reclining on a divan. Very sensual. Like her. Like the room.

A sleigh bed dominated the windowed wall. A comforter in an elegant paisley pattern of bold reds, cinnamon and gold lay atop it. Matching gold-fringed pillows were piled against the headboard invitingly. A mirrored dresser filled the wall space between the bedroom door and wardrobe. Tawny moved over to a large triple-wicked pillar candle on her dresser.

She turned to face him, smiling. "I told you I had plenty of candles."

She was even more beautiful with candlelight dancing across her face, flickering over her bare shoulders, casting the valley between her breasts into a mysterious shadowy place he longed to explore. Her smile faded and the perfume of the candles wafted around them, exotic scents that conjured images of hot sex, that stripped away his reserve and left him a man who ached for the woman he wanted and couldn't have. Her lips parted and he could have sworn he glimpsed a reciprocal heat in her eyes.

"You shouldn't burn them all. We don't have any idea how long the lights will be out." Nothing like a little censure to dissipate a mood.

"I have plenty. I've got a thing for candles."

"What else do you have a thing for?" he asked, his tongue moving faster under the circumstances than his internal censor. And he was only human. They were alone in her apartment, in candlelight, her bed was right there and less than five feet separated them.

She wet her lips, as if her mouth was suddenly too dry and he felt another stab of familiar guilt—this time for making her uncomfortable. "That was a joke. My misguided attempt at humor. Do you have a radio with batteries so we can find out what's going on out there?" Definitely time to introduce the real world. He needed outside stimuli to keep from drifting off into another fantasy of just the two of them.

"My boom box uses batteries." She opened her closet door and stepped over the pile of clothes on the floor. She knelt down and bent over. He should look away, direct his attention to the painting on the wall, check out the dark New York skyline. Hell, watching paint dry would be better, far more noble, than staring at her on her knees with her amazing, enticing, drool-inspiring bum in the air.

She backed out of the closet, boom box in hand, and stood. She flipped the switch. Nothing happened. "Okay. Batteries that aren't dead would be a bonus." She upended the radio on the bed and opened the battery compartment. "Six C-cell batteries. I'll have us fixed up in no time. I keep extras on hand."

She rounded the bed to the bedside drawer where he stood. She pulled out two batteries and tossed them onto the bed. She dug a bit more, pulling out a third. "Three isn't going to do it."

Her skin glimmered in the soft light, her eyes were soft and luminous, her scent issued a siren's call. He thrust his hands in his pockets to keep from reaching for her. He'd been mad to agree to be here tonight. "No. I'd say it's rather obvious we need three more."

"I've got it covered." Her smile said she was tired of him being a jerk. And he was tired of being a jerk, but it was better than giving in to his impulse to ease her onto the bed, peel her clothes off and become intimately acquainted with every delectable inch of her naked body.

She delved back into the drawer—obviously command central in her bedroom—and pulled out…the biggest vibrator he'd ever seen. Well, actually, he

didn't believe he'd ever seen a vibrator firsthand before. It was quite…large.

"Simon, meet Tiny." Tiny was pretty intimidating
from a man's point of view. Not that he suddenly felt
inadequate or anything. She unscrewed the bottom,
dropped two batteries out and replaced the top. She
put it back in the drawer and then pulled out a much
smaller dildo with a smaller stem on the top of it.
"This is Enrico and Bob." She waved the toy in his
general direction.

"Um, I gather the little guy is Bob because he…"

"Yep. You got it. He bobs up and down."

Simon reminded himself to breathe—but not too
heavily. This was going great. He should've abandoned her, along with his principles, and gotten the
hell out of her apartment when he'd had the opportunity. He'd only thought it was hot before. He was
burning up now. "I guess this answers the question
as to what else you have a thing for."

She pulled out a single battery and tossed it onto
the bed atop the others. "There you go. Six C-cell
batteries, and I promise they're all in working order.
Why don't you put them in?"

3

MAYBE SHE'D GONE A TAD too far introducing her vibrator boys by name, but she'd had enough of his quiet sarcasm and disapproval. According to Elliott, Simon's demeanor stemmed from being first-generation American. His father, a Brit, had relocated to New York before Simon was born to curate some museum or another. She didn't care if his father was next in line for the British throne, she was tired of Simon's hot-and-cold attitude. And if she was honest with herself, she was none too pleased with herself that he turned her on to the nth degree and annihilated her composure. Around him she couldn't seem to think of anything beyond sex. With him. She'd nearly made a fool of herself when he'd put his hands on her shoulders. And then when he'd touched her breast…she'd come close to begging him to take her then and there, hard and fast, against the wall, in the hallway. Simon brought out a sensuality in her that she'd never known before and in some aspects frightened her with its intensity.

Silently Simon loaded the batteries into her boom

box. His hands weren't quite steady as he fumbled with the last one. Maybe the close confines were getting to him, too.

The radio blared to life. "...so, it looks like it's a good old-fashioned blackout brought on by the incredible demand for a little air-conditioned relief from the triple-digit heat. Unfortunately, the lights are out across the Tristate area and authorities tell us they're not sure when they'll have the lights back on. It looks like it's going to be a hot night, so just settle down where you are and stay put. In honor of the blackout, we're going to open the lines for requests and dedications that have to do with hot and summer. And I guess we'll be seeing a bunch of newborns nine months from now. Hey, you've got to pass the time somehow. Let's start this set with an oldie, 'Love The One You're With'." Tawny reached over and turned it off.

Trapped in her apartment with Simon for the night? Tawny bit back her panic. Danger signals exploded in her brain—her, Simon, candlelight—and already it felt as if the temperature in her apartment had increased a few degrees.

"Well, we can forget take-out Thai. Are you hungry?" Sure, leave it to the fat girl to bring up food, but dammit, she was starving. And it took her mind off sex. And Simon. And sex with Simon. Well, probably not, but she was still hungry.

He grinned and she was totally disarmed by the

flash of his white teeth in the dim lighting. "I'm famished. I could chew nails."

"I don't keep much food on hand. There's a deli a block and a half away. Do you think it would still be open?"

"It should. During the 2003 blackout, food stores were selling out because they didn't know how long their power would be out. Better to sell it than let it ruin. I've even got some cash on me. Let's give it a go." He smiled with a touch of self-conscious eagerness. "And I wouldn't mind burning a roll or two of film."

Duh. He was a photographer. Of course he'd like to be taking pictures. And it was incredible how his whole demeanor changed when he talked about photography.

"Sure. Food and photographs. Works for me," she said.

No sooner had the words left her mouth than lightning flashed and thunder boomed overhead. Rain fell in a sudden onslaught. Nothing, it seemed, was subtle or happening in small measure tonight.

"Or not. Okay. That's it. I'm not planning anything else tonight because everything I plan gets trashed," she said with a nervous laugh. They were stuck here. She picked up a small votive to lead the way back down the hall. "I'm not a culinary queen, but nails shouldn't be necessary," she said.

She didn't comment when Simon blew out the other candles in the room before he picked up the ra-

Jennifer LaBrecque 47

dio and followed her. She had enough candles in the
closet to carry them for a week, but it wasn't worth
arguing the point.

She was more than willing to bury the hatchet between them since they were stuck here together.

She snagged her wineglass on the way into the
kitchen. "Good wine is a terrible thing to waste."

"Ah, something we agree on." Tawny waited for
Simon to exchange the radio for his glass and the
wine bottle. Given the minimum square footage of
her apartment, they'd have no trouble hearing the radio from the kitchen. He followed her into the other
room. Within a few seconds, several candles illuminated her galley kitchen.

"What's that?" Simon asked. She followed his
gaze to the top of the fridge. In the semidarkness,
Peaches resembled a blob of prey more than a feline.

"Peaches, my cat. He likes the top of the refrigerator. He's the one with a bad attitude and selective
hearing."

"Poor fella. You'd have a bad attitude, too, if you
were a guy called Peaches." Simon made a sympa-
thetic noise in the back of his throat and surprised
Tawny by reaching up to scratch the cat behind the
ears. Peaches promptly hissed and swatted.

"He's not Mister Friendly."

"Neither am I," Simon said with a self-deprecat-
ing smile as he leaned back against the counter and
crossed his arms over his chest.

"Well, forget it, I'm not adopting you if you find yourself abandoned," she said with a teasing smile, despite the flutter in her tummy at the thought of making Simon her own. "You'd probably be as bad-tempered and ungrateful as he is."

"Duly noted," he said with another smile that doubled her heart rate. "Why do you keep the wretch?"

"Because it was love at first sight on my part." She glanced away from him. That almost sounded as if she had declared herself in love with Simon at first sight. A totally ridiculous notion. "He'll come around sooner or later."

Simon quirked a sardonic brow in the direction of Peaches. "I believe you're an eternal optimist."

"Call me Pollyanna." She opened the refrigerator door and peered into the black hole, considering their limited food options. "The microwave or the oven won't work. I've got leftover pizza. And I can throw together a fruit salad. How does that sound?"

"Better than nails."

Tawny laughed, enjoying his quiet teasing and relaxing into his company. She pulled out the food and closed the fridge door. "Are you always so gracious and enthusiastic?"

"Yes, except when I'm in a bad mood." He sipped his wine, and as if the camaraderie between them was unacceptable, she could almost see him retreating. She wanted him to stay. "It was monumental bad timing that I wasn't the one delayed and Elliott isn't here with you instead."

Elliott. Right. Her fiancé. She twisted her ring with her thumb. Guilt flooded her. She hadn't spared Elliott a nominal thought since his phone call. She shrugged. "It's an emergency. We all do the best we can. I'm sure Elliott would rather not be trapped in the gallery with that acrylics guy. And while you might not be thrilled to be here, it's better than being stuck on the subway."

She pulled out the chopping board, a knife and a bowl.

"And why would you think I'm not thrilled to be here?" he asked.

She went to work chunking the fresh pineapple. She almost said she wasn't as dumb as she must look but thought better of it. "Should I believe you're thrilled to be stuck in this apartment with me?"

"Would you believe me if I told you there was no other place I'd rather be?" Something in the depths of his eyes stole her breath.

She laughed to cover her breathlessness and cored an apple. "No. I think there's probably a list a mile long of places you'd rather be, but you're too nice to say so."

"Quite. I'm such a nice guy."

"Be honest. Wouldn't you rather be at your girlfriend's? Or if the photo shoot had gone a little longer, you'd be with Chloe." Okay, she admitted it.

She was fishing. They'd double dated several times with Simon. Each time it had been a different woman. But after the photo shoot, Simon had always begged off whenever Elliott invited him along.

She added diced apple to the bowl and reached for a banana. His love life intrigued her. Not that it had anything to do with her. But if she was having head-banging sex with him in her dreams, she could at least know about his love life.

"I don't have a girlfriend and Chloe isn't my type," he said, shrugging. A thin, beautiful model wasn't his type? She looked at him considering the implications. Maybe he was...

"And no, I don't mean not my type that way. I'm not gay. Chloe's a nice woman, but she doesn't do a thing for me."

Whew! She shouldn't be so relieved. She sectioned an orange. What kind of woman was his type? Who would appeal to a self-contained man like Simon? And why didn't he have a girlfriend? In a dark, fiendish way, he was spine-tingling, toe-curling sexy. "So, what kind of woman does something for you?"

"I've never really thought about it."

"Sure you have. Everyone has a type they go for," she said.

"I don't really have a type."

He seriously needed to loosen up a bit. She mixed the fruit together. "Sure you do. I bet if you stop and think about it, there's a certain type of woman that attracts you, that makes your blood run a little hotter."

"Is this some kind of game, Tawny? Do you want me to say it's a woman like you?" His voice was low, dangerous in its quiet intensity.

Wasn't that exactly what she wanted? To know that for all the times she'd writhed, screamed his name in the middle of an orgasm, woken up wet and spent, that he wasn't totally immune to her? Yes and no. The only game she was playing was with herself, and it was a dangerous one. She looked away from his dark-eyed gaze, glad to busy herself with getting two bowls out of her cabinet. "Don't be ridiculous. You've made it abundantly clear how you regard me. I'm just surprised you're not still seeing Lenore. You made a nice couple." Lenore had been Simon's date the night Elliott had proposed. The tall, willowy blonde had been a perfect complement to Simon's urbane dark looks.

She divvied out the portions and they sat at the small wrought-iron table she'd tucked in the corner.

Simon shrugged. "Lenore is nice. That's why I quit seeing her. I'm in a bit of an unrequited love and it didn't seem fair to date her when my head and heart were otherwise engaged. Delicious, by the way," he said, indicating the fruit and pizza. "Thank you."

"Glad you like it." His other words slammed into her. A dark jealousy coiled through her at the thought of a woman capturing the distant Simon's heart. This mystery woman must be a paragon. Beautiful, sophisticated, thin, witty, probably a couple of Ph.D.s under her belt. Unwisely, unwittingly, instinctively Tawny hated her. Hated her for capturing his heart and hated her for tossing it aside.

So of course she said, "I'm sorry. That's a hard place to be. Do you want to talk about it? About her? Sometimes talking it over with someone, things aren't as hopeless as they seem." She couldn't seem to shut up, hell-bent on atoning for her lust. "Maybe I could help you figure out a way to win her over— you know, another woman's perspective."

She bit into the pizza, finding something else to do with her mouth other than babble on. Simon regarded her over the rim of his wineglass, his expression indecipherable. "You're offering aid with my dismal love life?"

It could prove to be just the cure she needed to get over this…thing for him. She nodded and swallowed. "Sure. Why not?"

He placed his empty glass on the table. "That's generous, but she's unavailable."

Ouch. "She's married?"

"No. But she's in a serious relationship."

That merely irritated her. Was Simon truly in love or was it the unavailability factor? People, especially men, always wanted what they couldn't have. Put a taboo label on it and they had to have it.

"Until she says *I do,* she's not unavailable. You've

got to decide how important she is to you. If you're willing to forego other relationships, she must matter a lot. Wake up, Simon, and smell the coffee. What're you gonna do? Sit around in some weird celibate state—"

"I never mentioned celibacy." Simon tried to pull a haughty look on her.

Tawny rolled her eyes. "Give me a break. If you won't date a woman because you don't want to be unfair, then you're certainly not sleeping with anyone." Alarming how much that pleased her. So of course she worked even harder to push him. "You're gonna moon around in a celibate state for a couple of years or even the rest of your life because she's in a relationship but not married? How bad do you want her?"

"With every fiber of my being."

His quiet intensity sent a shiver down her spine and pierced her heart. What was wrong with her? Who he wanted and how much he wanted her had nothing to do with Tawny.

"Then it's time for you to fish or cut bait."

"THANKS FOR YOUR ADVICE to the lovelorn. I'll keep the 'fish or cut bait' in mind."

Wasn't that twisted? The object of his unrequited affection—and hence intense guilt, as she was engaged to his best friend—sat across the table, bathed in candlelight, wearing a sexy halter top and shorts and advising him to put a move on her. At least, that's what he'd interpreted her charming colloquialism to mean.

Tawny topped off her wineglass and refilled his at the same time. "Well, I think you should go for it. What have you got to lose?"

What did he have to lose if he went for *her* right now? "Really nothing, other than those small matters of pride and self-esteem."

"It's pretty hard to wrap your arms around those and snuggle up to them. Or enjoy a glass of wine or a candlelit bubble bath with them either."

He struggled to keep his expression one of sardonic amusement while inside her words played out in his head as snapshots of the two of them. The irony of sharing a glass of wine with her in candlelight nearly slayed him. He was an absolute masochist to participate in this conversation. Bugger that, he was a masochist to even *be* here.

"But a glass of wine sooner or later is gone, eventually the candles burn out, and the water grows cold, so perhaps one has to make the more long-lasting choice."

"Except that life is fleeting. Tomorrow may not come before the wine stops flowing or the water cools."

"Am I in the company of a hedonist?" he asked, very clearly recalling his recent introduction to Tiny, Enrico and Bob, her on-demand boyfriends.

She tucked a piece of hair behind her ear. "Life is

short and it's a shame to waste opportunities. This woman could be the love of your life and you're letting her slip away. And who knows? She may feel the same way about you." He really was a pathetic sod. He was flattered she didn't consider him so repugnant she couldn't imagine a woman attracted to him. "Maybe she just doesn't know it yet. Or she could be shy and afraid to tell you."

Simon laughed. Neither of those came to mind in a Tawny word-association exercise. Other than her aversion to the dark, she'd never displayed either characteristic. "I don't think shy or fear are factors when it comes to my lady."

Tawny leaned her elbow on the table and pursed her lips, tapping one finger against the corner of her mouth as she eyed him consideringly. She had a truly lovely mouth, full but without the collagen bloat so popular these days.

"Well, maybe this is some kind of courtly love." She snapped her fingers. "That's it. You know, chivalry and all. Knights only loved their ladies from afar. Maybe you're just afraid to declare yourself because you aren't truly physically attracted to her. Maybe you wouldn't know what to do with her if she actually reciprocated your attraction," she said. She crossed her arms as if she'd neatly solved a little puzzle.

His boyhood days of envisioning himself as a bold knight were long gone. There was nothing courtly or chivalrous about the maelstrom of emotion she evoked in him. He absolutely burned for her. And he'd had enough of her speculation. It was time for this conversation to end. He knew one sure way to kill the conversation and prove to her just how far removed he was from her romanticized notions.

He traced his finger along the edge of his glass and smiled at her across the table, offering her a glimpse of the dark passion seething beneath his surface. "I don't know about courtly love." He chose his next words very deliberately—crude and base—to make a point. "I do know I would fuck her senseless for a week, given half a chance."

Her eyes grew huge and she swallowed hard, but she didn't look away. "Oh. Senseless…a week…well, then."

Okay. Perhaps he'd gone a bit over the top there. "I apologize if I shocked you."

She raised her chin. "I'm not shocked at all. I think all that passion is…well, hot. I'm not sure there's a woman alive who wouldn't want to know a man was so hot for her he'd like to—" she paused and emphasized the very words he'd uttered "—fuck her senseless for a week. As long as somewhere in the week he wanted to work a little conversation and getting to know her into the sexathon."

Far from offensive, it sounded sexy and exciting when she threw his words back at him. Especially when she drawled it in that low, honeyed tone with a glint in her eye that spoke more to interest and arousal.

Simon was knee-deep in muck but apparently lacked enough sense to stop wading. "I've never operated solely from a state of lust. Her brain and her personality are half the appeal. Otherwise I'd only want her for half a week. And I wouldn't worry about senseless."

Her naughty smile wrecked him. "You are wicked, Simon Thackeray."

Forget muck. This felt like dangerous sexual flirting and he needed to stop. And he would. Soon. He leaned forward, drawn by the heat in her eyes, lured by her smile. "Perhaps my love languishes unrequited because I'm too wicked to love."

She shifted forward, her knee brushed his and the contact surged through him. A seductive smile curved her lush mouth. "I seriously doubt that. Don't you know that all that wickedness just drives women to distraction?"

All he truly knew was that she drove him beyond distraction. Beyond caution. "Are you speaking from personal experience?"

"The last time I checked, I was a woman, so I suppose so." There was something in her eyes. Something that said she knew how utterly wicked he could be and she liked it, despite herself.

Which was ridiculous because he'd been very careful to limit his exposure to her. He raised his brow in question. As if she suddenly realized what he'd seen in her eyes, she blinked and it vanished. She leaned back into her chair, putting a distance that existed beyond mere space between them. Thank God one of them had some sense. "What do you do with all of that pent-up…energy?"

Egad, the woman was relentlessly curious—no trouble at all believing she got herself locked into a wardrobe—which was yet one more reason he'd taken himself out of her and Elliott's sphere. For one moment he considered telling her he jerked off often, just to see if it would shock her into no more questions, but that tactic had already failed once. And quite simply he couldn't bring himself to be so crude. He opted for the truth.

"I run. A lot. At this point, I'm probably hovering in marathon-training range." He laughed at himself. "And never underestimate the efficiency of the proverbial cold shower."

As it stood now, a cold shower sounded better and better on more than one count. Sweat slicked him and her skin glistened with a fine sheen of moisture. He was a sick beast when a woman sweating struck him as sexy.

"I didn't know you were a runner. I'm nowhere close to marathon training, but I run five days a week."

"Are you sexually frustrated, as well?" He might as well be hung for a sheep as a lamb.

"No. I have a fat ass," she said with a cheeky grin

that held a smidgen of self-consciousness. He bit back the protest that her ass was perfect, enticing and far from fat. She went on, "We should run together some time."

Somehow running with her to relieve the stress of Tawny-induced lust seemed self-defeating and warped. He liked it. "Maybe we should."

"How about tomorrow?" she said.

Depending on how long it took to restore the power, he'd definitely need it.

"It's a date then." Poor word choice. "I didn't mean a date as in a *date*." Yet another reason he avoided being around her. His brain seemed to become nothing more than rat turds rolling around in his empty head when she was near.

She raised her eyebrows. Amusement at his verbal bumbling danced in her eyes and twitched at her lips. "I knew what you meant."

From the other room her cell phone rang. She scraped her chair back, excusing herself.

Simon stayed in the kitchen to offer her some privacy. He began to clear the table. Without the hum of the refrigerator, the AC and all the other white noise associated with electricity, he couldn't help but overhear her conversation, even with the radio on.

"Yes, Mom, I'm fine…. No, he's not here. He got caught at the gallery…. No. I'm not alone. One of Elliott's friends stopped by…. Yes. He's a photographer…. No, they don't know when they'll have it back on…. No. No sign of looting or vandalism, but yes, we're going to stay in." Her voice lowered. "Mom, improper isn't the same here as it is at home. And I'd rather not be alone…. Yes, I'll call you later."

Elliott had flown down to meet Tawny's parents after the engagement and given Simon an earful afterward. Very conservative, very Southern, very proper. Rarified members of the genteel Savannah blue-blood set, her father was a surgeon and her mother was a lifetime member of the garden club. They'd lunched at the country club.

It took less than a thimbleful of imagination to figure out Mama Edwards had reprimanded Tawny over the impropriety of being alone in her apartment during a blackout with another man. God help them both if her mother had overheard their conversation. And at least her mum called to check on her. Simon doubted he'd even crossed his parents' minds. He'd been off their radar screen since he left home. Who was he fooling? He'd never registered *on* their radar screen.

Tawny walked back into the kitchen just as he finished rinsing and stacking the bowls. "My mother," she confirmed. "They heard about it on CNN." She took in the tidied kitchen. "You cleaned up! If I weren't already taken, I'd keep you for myself."

Her teasing words were a dagger to his heart.

"Ah, but there is Elliott, isn't there?" He deliberately chilled his tone.

"Yes, there is Elliott." She put her cell phone on the counter and turned to him. "But that reminds me, exactly why were you and Elliott coming over this evening?"

4

SIMON HAD GROWN UP IN New York City and had never seen an actual deer caught in headlamps, but he experienced a sudden onset of empathy. Bugger. If he'd been thinking with his whole brain instead of sniffing about after Tawny like some lust-driven horn dog, he would've seen this coming, should've anticipated the question. Instead she'd figuratively caught him with his trousers down. Simon didn't feel like a very bright boy.

"It's a bit of a mystery to me." He was a terrible liar.

"Uh-huh."

She clearly didn't believe him. And he might stretch the truth to protect her from what he perceived to be Elliott's selfishness, but he couldn't knowingly lie to her. However, exactly how Elliott planned to handle this impending fiasco *was* a mystery to him.

She picked up her cell phone. "Let's call Elliott. It's not as if he's busy or anything if he's locked in the gallery without electricity."

Simon winced inside. She'd be devastated to know just how *busy* Elliott might be at the moment.

Tawny speed dialed the number and drummed her fingers on the counter.

"Hi, Elliott. Everything quiet over there? Fine… Nothing. We ate cold pizza and fruit. I asked Simon what it was you wanted to talk about tonight. Apparently he's as in the dark as I am…. No, I didn't intend that as a pun…. So let's talk now…. I know you wanted to be here, but you might as well tell me over the phone, because you've aroused my curiosity. Don't make me wait. You've got to satisfy me."

Aroused…wait any longer…satisfy me. She talked to Elliot this way and he still got off on someone else? That told Simon all he needed to know about his friend. Since Elliott wasn't dead, he must be gay.

"Yes. He's right here. Okay." She huffed out a breath and handed the phone across to Simon. "He wants to talk to you."

Simon reluctantly took the phone.

Tawny planted her hands on her hips and glared at him. Brilliant. Forget a private conversation. Not that he blamed her. She had to feel jerked around.

Instinct told him he wasn't going to like where this was headed. "Elliott?"

"Tawny wants to know what I wanted to talk to her about." Elliott sounded positively panicked.

Simon leaned against the counter and crossed one foot over the other. "Right."

"I can't tell her over the phone," Elliott said as if Simon had demanded he do that very thing.

Simon braved a glance at Tawny's set features. "I don't believe there's a choice."

"But there is." He recognized Elliott's wheedling enthusiastic tone. Whatever it was, Simon's instincts were already screaming *no*. "The right choice. You tell her."

Simon damn near dropped the phone. "No."

"Yes. The more I think about it, this works out better."

Maybe for Elliott. Cold day in hell and all that.

"Absolutely not."

"Oh, come on, Si. You two already don't like one another. And what else are you going to talk about? What have you got to do stuck there in the dark with one another? This blackout could last several hours."

"Not a chance."

"Think about it. It'd be better this way." Was it only twelve hours ago that he'd declared nothing Elliott did could compromise their friendship? He was rethinking that position. "You don't know Tawny the way I do. She's not going to give up on this until one of us tells her. I can try feeding her some line about wedding plans, but when she finds out the truth, that's just going to make it a thousand times worse."

"I don't see why your conversation can't wait."

"I'm telling you, she's sexy and sweet but beneath

those soft curves and big green eyes she's relentless when she wants something. She's a steel magnolia."

Simon recognized that truth. He'd experienced it firsthand when she'd sunk her teeth into the topic of his love life. He considered banging his head against the counter or perhaps the cabinet. Anything solid would do.

Could this night possibly get any better? First he was trapped with a woman he wanted beyond reason. Now said woman was about to hound him to no end for news sure to crush her. And he was the lucky devil doing double duty. Not only was he in the firing line to be shot as the messenger, but who else was around to endure the messy aftermath? And when it was all said and done, he'd wade through hell and back if he thought she needed him.

"I'll take care of it."

"Simon, you are the best friend a man could have."

"We'll talk about that later." This wasn't for Elliott. This was for Tawny. Because she deserved better than hearing the truth over the phone while Elliott was locked in with his new lover. Because it might render him asunder, but he would give her a strong shoulder to cry on and be there for her.

"Okay. I'm grateful. Eternally grateful. Let me talk to Tawny for a minute."

Silently Simon passed the phone back to Tawny.

"Yes?… He is?… Okay. Stay safe and I'll talk to you later," she said. She flipped the cell phone closed, disconnecting the call. She picked up her glass and polished it off. Putting the empty goblet on the counter, she looked at Simon expectantly, some of her former exasperation lingering in her eyes and the set of her mouth.

"I understand you have something to tell me?"

Apprehension knotted Simon's gut. The proverbial shit was about to hit the proverbial fan.

"Let's go in the other room. You'll want to sit down for this."

SIMON LOOKED GRIM. SO MUCH for the let's-all-jump-in-bed ménage-à-trois theory, although she already pretty much knew that was toast. What could possibly warrant that rigid, resigned set to his jaw, and was that a flash of *pity* in his eyes when he looked at her?

The truth slammed her. She sucked in a calming breath. Elliott was dying. He'd been handed down some awful diagnosis and the two of them were going to break the news to her. She was the worst human being possible, having erotic dreams about Simon and wallowing in a private lustfest while poor, brave Elliott faced the specter of death alone.

Simon leaned forward, bracing his arms on his knees, his fingers linked together. He turned to face her. "Elliott should be the one telling you…. I was only coming to lend moral support…. I'm not sure where to begin."

Tawny squared her shoulders and sat straighter on her end of the sofa. She'd be brave. "How long has he known?"

Simon did a double take. "How long have *you* known?"

"Well, just now."

Simon slanted a questioning look her way. "Now?"

"I figured it out and Elliott can count on me to stand by him, even if the wedding doesn't happen." He might be too sick or he just might not have enough time to make it to the altar.

"Tawny, what is it that you think you know?"

"Elliott's dying, isn't he? What is it? Cancer? A tumor? How long does he have? I knew he'd been acting different lately, but I thought…"

Simon waved a hand, stilling her. "Let's back up a bit. You think Elliott's dying?"

"Isn't he? You look like the Grim Reaper."

"I always look like the Grim Reaper." Simon sighed. "As far as I know, Elliott's healthy as a horse." *Whew.* She sagged against the sofa, limp with relief. As long as Elliott was healthy, nothing could… "He's been seeing someone else."

What? She shot up. "Bastard." She'd kill him. Here she'd been feeling guilty over *dreams,* when all the while Elliott was playing Bury the Bone with someone else. "Is it someone I know?"

"I think you've met him."

It took a few seconds for the definitive *him* to

soak through her haze of shock and anger. "Him? Did you just say *him,* as in Elliott's seeing a *guy?*"

Simon offered a curt nod. "That's what he told me this morning."

"A man? A man! I've been dumped for a freaking man?" Another woman was bad enough, but a man? She'd never been so angry and humiliated in her life. And don't forget betrayed.

The hot press of tears gathered. Dammit. She didn't get really mad that often, but when she did, instead of ranting and raving she cried. It sucked.

Simon shook his head. "I don't think he necessarily wants to break up. He just wanted to come clean. He says it's only been once and he thinks he's bisexual." Simon looked grimmer than ever.

Elliott's nerve floored her. He didn't necessarily want to break up? That was rich. And it fueled her anger. She didn't have anything against homosexuals, but she wasn't marrying one. She tugged at the ring on her finger. It stuck on her knuckle. That was the final detail that totally unhinged her. Tawny, the family screwup, had once again managed to not get it right. Her anger spilled over in the form of hot tears rolling down her cheeks. She tugged again. Finally she yanked the ring off. She shoved it into Simon's hand. "I won't be needing this any longer." The last word ended on a sob.

She was so angry she was shaking. And blubbering. Simon slid across the space separating them. She caught a glimpse of his face. He looked positively stricken. He folded her into his arms, pulling her against the wall of his chest, cradling her, rocking her back and forth. "Please don't cry, Tawny. It's going to be okay."

Stern, austere, sarcastic Simon offered her solace. That this man who didn't like her very well was reduced to having to comfort her went a long way in cooling her anger and stemming her tears. Crying when she was angry had proven a curse of embarrassment since childhood.

That was almost as humiliating as her being inadequate enough to send Elliott to seek male companionship. She ought to have some measure of pride and pull away, but somehow it felt less embarrassing to simply stay where she was, pressed against Simon's chest. Plus it was a very nice chest.

"How amusing for me to offer you advice on your love life when mine was down the toilet and I didn't even have enough sense to know it," she said against his shirt. "How pathetic."

"Tawny, never refer to yourself again as *pathetic*." He cupped her face in his hands and tilted her head back until she looked at him. He gentled away her tears with his thumbs. Her skin tingled beneath his touch. His jeans-clad knee pressed against her bare leg. "There is nothing remotely pathetic about you. You're beautiful and sexy."

Simon could obviously lie with the best of them.

She knew her eyes and nose were swollen from crying. Some women cried prettily. She wasn't one of them. She was fairly certain she wasn't looking her level best. And then there was the little matter of Elliott dipping his wick…definitely where it didn't belong. "Yes, I'm so beautiful and sexy, I drove my fiancé to being gay."

"Right now I'm very pissed with Elliott. And even though he's my friend, he's an idiot." He patted her awkwardly on her shoulder.

Poor Simon. Small wonder he'd been so reluctant to broach this subject. "It was bad enough that he stuck you in the middle. You don't have to say all of this. And don't worry, I'm through crying. When I get angry, I cry. Charming little quirk." She dashed away the last of her tears.

"Elliott is all kinds of a fool."

She sniffled. This was the man she'd seen the day he'd photographed her, the man she'd glimpsed behind the wall of reserve. He really could be very nice. "It's very chivalrous of you to say that."

"I don't have a chivalrous bone in my body. I'm stating the obvious. You're beautiful and sexy and Elliott's an idiot," Simon said.

Tawny opened her mouth to argue the point and Simon interrupted her.

"Perhaps this will convince you," he said, lowering his head and capturing her mouth.

TAWNY TASTED LIKE EXACTLY what she was—forbidden fruit. Sweet, hot, drugging, addictive. He felt her hesitation and surprise, tasted the brine of her tears.

Simon pulled away from her mouth and the temptation to plunder and explore. He raked his hand through his hair. "That was out of line. I apologize."

She shook her head. "No." She linked her arms around his neck and pulled his head back down to hers. "Please don't apologize," she said, her breath warming him. Her lips molded to his and a fantasy came to life. Tawny kissed him, hard and hot.

He knew she was angry with Elliott. Knew he was payback. Knew he should walk away. But while his head said one thing, his heart said another. God help him, he returned her kiss. Six months of pent-up passion unleashed within him. He'd lived with fantasies. And now he held the flesh-and-blood embodiment of those fantasies in his arms.

Her tongue probed at his lips and the last vestige of his resistence deserted him. He buried his hands in her hair and crushed her to him. She strained against him, her anger, her frustration almost palpable. And then it was gone, replaced by something less volatile—and far more dangerous. She softened, her mouth now giving rather than taking. Offering. He took and gave in return.

Simon slid his hands from her hair and stroked down the satin warmth of her bare shoulders. She moaned into his mouth and shuddered against him.

Reason took a holiday. He sank back onto the

couch and she followed him, lying against him, between his thighs. Her hips pressed against an erection he couldn't deny. Her fingers winnowed through his hair as he thoroughly explored the hot sweetness of her mouth. He plied his hands along the sexy curve of her back. He would love to photograph the lovely curve of her neck, bared by her upswept hair that led to the sinuous line of her back. He touched her with the reverence of an artist and the appreciation of a man.

The intensity of her kiss shook him. She pressed against his erection in supplication and he groaned into her mouth. He filled his hands with the full roundness of her buttocks and pulled her harder against him. She slid one leg over his, straddling his thigh, opening herself to him.

He ran his fingers along the silk of her thighs, his knuckles brushing against the edge of her panties. Oh, sweet heaven, they were wet.

"Oh, Simon," she moaned into his mouth, "you always make me…"

She provided a voice-activated sanity check. He wrenched away from her and steadied himself on one elbow, although she remained between his thighs. What the hell was he doing? He'd been one second away from slipping his finger beneath the elastic of her panties and touching her intimately. He gulped air and sought some measure of his control that had been woefully missing a few seconds ago.

Tawny remained atop him, her body pressed intimately against his. Her arousal, mingled with her perfume, was a heady scent.

"I'm sorry," he said. And just how sorry was he with one hand still on her delectable bottom? He jerked his hand away and rubbed his brow.

She scooted to the other end of the couch. He sat up, missing the press of her between his thighs, as if a vital part of him had been amputated.

Tears still clung to her lashes. Passion weighted her lids. His kisses had left her lips swollen and ripe.

"I'm really sorry," he repeated. "I didn't mean to…that shouldn't have…I got out of hand."

"Please don't apologize, Simon. You didn't exactly force yourself on me. I crawled on top of you." She looked away from him, throwing the fine line of her nose and the curve of her cheek into shadowy relief. "You must think I'm a slut."

He rubbed the back of his neck, contrite. He had the utmost respect for her—*slut* had never crossed his mind. He'd kissed her to *show* her how desirable she was, because *telling* hadn't worked. Instead he'd further compromised her self-esteem.

"Never. You were upset, I was out of line and it won't happen again. I never meant to take advantage of you."

She shook her head. "You didn't take advantage of me. I was the one out of line." She touched his hand and then jerked back when she realized what she'd done. "I don't want you to be uncomfortable. I won't throw myself at you again."

He almost pointed out that she should have a very good idea of just how much he'd enjoyed it since she had been riding the ridge of his erection. It had left him hard, but it had by no means posed a hardship. His body screamed that she could throw herself at him any day, any way, any time.

Tawny curled up, tucking one foot beneath her. She smoothed her fingers over the back of the couch. "Did you know about Elliott?"

Elliott. Much better than discussing that kiss. "No. On either count. He's never even hinted at being gay or at being interested in someone other than you."

Although maybe the signs had been there but Simon had been too obtuse to see them. Elliott was a bastard for cheating on her and dragging Simon into it, but Simon believed Elliott cared for Tawny. Right now she was hurt and betrayed, but she must still care for Elliott. As a friend, it was his role to ensure neither Tawny nor Elliott did anything rash regarding their future that they'd later regret. That's how a man of honor would behave.

She huffed out a breath. "I don't feel quite so stupid if you didn't have a clue either."

"I thought he was joking when he first told me."

"Well, I know he couldn't have possibly orchestrated a blackout, but how convenient for him. This way he could stick you with telling me, the scum-sucking son of a bitch."

He bit back a laugh. She definitely had a colorful way with the English language. He didn't want this woman pissed at him. "I know you're hurt. I would be, too. But in the morning you'll feel differently about all of this. You and Elliott can work this out."

She crossed her arms over her chest, which did incredible things to her already pretty damn incredible cleavage, and directed a haughty look his way.

"Why don't you ring him?" Simon tried again. He'd spent enough time around women to know that talking, venting, was a big deal. And Elliott, who avoided confrontation at every opportunity, certainly wasn't going to initiate a conversation. "Talk to him. I'll go in the other room and give you some privacy."

She threw up a staying hand, her nose in the air. "Not going to happen. I have nothing to say to Elliott. Well, maybe a thing or two, but not while he's there with his new lover." She shook her head. "No thanks. And I don't even want to think about what they're probably doing right now."

"That makes two of us," Simon said without thinking.

"And what's there to say other than he's a two-timer who better not have given me some communicable disease he picked up while he was out screwing around?"

"He says it was safe sex."

"I hope he's not lying about that," she said.

"No. I asked him bluntly."

"That's a relief. So other than the satisfaction of cussing him out, I don't need to talk to him. There's no going back and there's no going forward. We're playing on a whole different ball field now. I'd had some doubts in the last couple of weeks and this just nailed it."

Had she really been having doubts? His skepticism must've shown.

"I can tell what you're thinking. Sure that's a convenient way for me to save face, but it's true. Ever since I started having—" she stopped as if she'd almost said something she shouldn't "—well, second thoughts. And I've had an increasing sense of Elliott trying to shape me into what he wanted me to be."

Elliott had laughingly said once on a double date that he possessed a better sense of style than Tawny. Simon also recalled another comment that Elliott needed to take her shopping. Both times Simon had thought Elliott out of line and far off the mark. Simon liked her sense of style. He wasn't quite sure what to say. "Elliott has very specific ideas."

"Uh-huh. Trust me. My parents have been trying to mold me long enough. I recognize the signs. Regardless, Elliott and I are history."

Which left her a free agent and him still constrained by the bounds of friendship.

5

COULD SHE HAVE POSSIBLY made it any clearer than if she'd held up a sign inviting him to kiss her again? And again. And then take it further. To pick up where he'd left off, with his fingers brushing against her wet panties.

They both obviously wanted one another. He'd felt her damp underwear and she'd felt his rock-hard erection. And she'd just told him in no uncertain terms that she no longer had a future with Elliott.

Simon's hair stood up at the crown where she'd run her fingers through it. She rather liked it because it made him much less intimidating and proved him human.

"People say and do a lot of things they don't really mean when they're angry," he said in the tone of a peacemaker.

Was he implying she was irrational and should make allowances for Elliott's wandering penis? Ha. She was very much in touch with rational thought. "I'm not angry."

Simon simply looked at her.

"Okay. Maybe I'm still a little mad that he cheated on me and that it was with a man." She cringed inside, feeling fat, ugly, lacking and unwanted. "How can I even compete when I don't have the same equipment?"

Simon shook his head, a touch of anger marking his face and the movement. "You don't compete. As difficult as it might be to believe, this isn't about you."

Freaking easy for him to say. "Have you ever had a girlfriend tell you she'd discovered her inner lesbian after sex with you?"

"Uh, no."

"I didn't think so. Don't you think that might leave you feeling a little deficient? Like your equipment wasn't up to par or you had some serious operator error going on?"

Simon looked like a man facing a firing squad. "I know it feels that way, but this isn't because there's a problem with you. Elliott's the one with the problem. And I sure as hell wish he'd talked to me before he did something stupid that buggered up his relationship with you."

His vehemence and apparent disapproval of Elliott surprised her. Usually, right or wrong, men stuck together. And she'd always sensed Simon didn't like her, so his reaction doubly surprised her.

She picked a *People* magazine off the bamboo chest and fanned herself. "I'm surprised you don't think it's his lucky day that he's managed to get rid of me."

Simon sat ramrod straight. "I'm sorry you misunderstood my actions that way."

What? As if she was some neurotic she-devil who'd misinterpreted his friendly demeanor? She was pissed and hot and sweaty. He'd picked the wrong day and the wrong gal to pull that holier-than-thou crap. She stood, bracing one knee on the couch, and planted her hands on her hips.

"Whoa. Stop right there. You're sorry I misinterpreted your actions? If you're going to apologize, then do it right. If you're not, then save your breath. But don't even think about giving me some backhanded apology."

He had the grace to look slightly ashamed but still arrogant. And very sexy with the candlelight flickering from the table beside him. "You're right. I've acted like a jerk and I'm still acting like a jerk."

That surprised her. But then again, she never really knew quite what to expect from Simon. "I didn't call you a jerk. Not exactly. Well, maybe that's what I was implying." She'd had it with all the prevarication. What was the point? "Let's just cut to the chase. You've never liked me. You've barely managed to be civil and I've never known why. I thought that day you photographed me it was different…I thought… well, never mind. I'm a big girl, and after finding out that my fiancé prefers men, I don't suppose it can get any worse. So while we're sitting here with nothing else to do, why don't you enlighten me? Tell me why you've never liked me. They say confession is good for the soul."

"I don't think…"

"Oh, come on, Simon. Get real. There's something about the dark of night that brings out the daring. You know how it is. Things you'd never think about in the light of day. Things you'd never do or say otherwise somehow seem okay in the dark."

Their hot kiss—her tongue in his mouth and his hands on her ass, pulling her harder into his erection—still lingered between them. She saw it in his face. "We both know I've never had the guts to ask before and I probably won't have the guts to ask again. In fact, after tonight our paths probably won't cross again. So let's get daring in the dark and have a real conversation," she said.

The idea of not seeing Simon again was far more disquieting than the thought of not seeing Elliott again. She was needling Simon, but it was better than flinging herself at him. What she really wanted to do was lose herself in his arms, feel the heavy thud of his heart beneath hers, taste the heat of his passion, wallow in the desire that left her aching, wet and feeling like a desirable woman. She longed to discover firsthand whether the real passion between them was as potent and incredible as her dreams.

"If our paths won't cross again, what could it possibly matter?" he said. The flickering light played tricks on her. For a brief second she could've sworn dismay flashed in his eyes.

"Because it'll bother me until I have an answer. My nickname growing up was Bulldog because I can't let things go. Why you disliked me will niggle at the back of my mind and worry me—unfinished business—until ten years from now I have to track you down and demand an answer so I can take myself off Prozac."

Simon frowned in confusion. "You're on an antidepressant?"

Tawny smiled at him. It was sort of weird trying to charm a man into telling you why he disliked you. But nothing about the feelings Simon stirred in her was normal or comfortable. Between Simon and Elliott, her journey of self-discovery had taken an abrupt turn. "No. But if you don't give me an answer, it'll drive me crazy and I'll have to start taking it. So go ahead and exoncrate yourself up front."

He shook his head but seemed to relax, stretching his arm along the couch back. He had nice arms. Just the right amount of muscle and a smattering of dark hair. Who was she kidding? Everything about him registered on her sexy meter. And—woohoo—she didn't have to feel guilty about it anymore. She could lust up front and outright without even a twinge of conscience.

"Does everyone in your family communicate this way?" he asked.

"No." She laughed and tossed the ball right back at him. "Does everyone in your family try to dodge the issue by introducing another topic?"

He grinned and a healthy dose of that guilt-free lust slammed her. "No. They simply don't talk."

It was the most he'd ever said about his family and she was curious to know more. "The British stiff upper lip?"

"Something like that. And their heads are full of ancient artifacts and civilizations." Per Elliott, his father was a museum curator and his mother was an archaeology—or maybe it was anthropology—professor. "They find the modern world something of an inconvenience."

It took a nanosecond for her to feel the loneliness of a little boy who had always hovered on the periphery of his parents' attention. Tawny knew as surely as she knew her name that Simon had been something of an inconvenience, as well. She related. "I wasn't an inconvenience, but I've always been a disappointment."

"I never said I was an inconvenience."

"You didn't have to say it."

He tilted his head to one side. "How could your parents possibly find you a disappointment?"

Okay. So he was probably just looking to shift the conversation from himself, but he seemed genuinely puzzled that she might disappoint Dr. and Mrs. Carlton Jonathan Edwards III.

"It's been all too easy. I'm not exactly the overachiever my sister Sylvia is—magna cum laude from Yale and a rising member of the Savannah bar." Out of nervous habit she started to twist her ring on her finger and realized it was no longer there. Her nail scraped her bare finger. "Betsy, my younger sister, married one of daddy's partner's sons. She and Tad have a beautiful home on Wilmington Island in a prestigious gated community. Me? I'm not as smart as Sylvia and I'm not as refined and gracious as Betsy. I talk too much, I'm too assertive, I have a master's degree in business but I plan parties for a living. I committed the ultimate sin of leaving Savannah, Georgia. When I came home with Elliott, they were pleased, although he wasn't a Southerner. Now it turns out he's gay."

She was batting a thousand here. And while she was hauling all of her shortcomings out for examination… "Oh, yeah, and Sylvia and Betsy take after my parents who are tall and thin. Thanks to recessive genes, I take after Grandmother Burdette, short with a big butt." And add talking too much and saying the wrong thing to that list. Why the heck had she mentioned her big ass?

Simon crossed his arms over his chest, restrained strength in lean, sinewy muscle. He leveled an uncompromising look at her from his end. "Are you sure you want the truth, here in the dark?"

Uh-oh. Something in his tone reminded her of Nicholson in *A Few Good Men*, assuring them they couldn't handle the truth. She'd asked for it, but now she wasn't so certain she wanted it. But she'd never run away from things or buried her head in the sand, and she wouldn't start now. "Absolutely."

"If that's really how your parents feel, all of you need to get over it. Lose the pity party and look at things the way they really are. You say you're a party planner as if it's some lesser accomplishment. You're an event planner for a law firm with a hundred and fifty practicing attorneys. According to Elliott, you do an incredible job planning and executing a multitude of functions. That requires tremendous organizational and negotiation skills."

She opened her mouth to point out she had an assistant, but he forestalled her with a raised hand.

"Let me finish and then the floor's yours. I think you came to New York to get away from your parents' censure, but you might as well pack up and go home if you're going to continue to see yourself through their eyes and judge yourself against some mythical standard." *Ouch.* His tone softened. "You'll never be free to be you until you accept and like who you are. I don't know what your sisters look like and I don't care. Your body would drop most men to their knees. Any man with half a dose of testosterone would tell you that you have the perfect behind. I'd like to think men aren't quite so shallow as to fall in love with your behind and overlook all of your other obvious attributes and qualities, but certainly any man would love your derriere. It could drive a man to madness."

Well. It was her turn to talk and she didn't know what to say. He'd certainly taken her at her word and said a lot. And perhaps he was right. She'd ostensibly moved to the Big Apple to shake off the confines and constraints of Savannah aristocracy, but was she still measuring herself against their standards? And how much of her attraction to Elliott and her subsequent engagement was due to the need for their elusive approval? And she'd think about all of that. Later. Now her fragile, wounded, her-fiancé-succumbed-to-the-charms-of-a-man ego latched on to the part about her body dropping a man to his knees and her ass driving him to madness. "Really? Madness?"

He quirked an eyebrow at her as if to say he knew where she was coming from and then he smiled at her, the first smile she'd ever received from him that actually reached his eyes. Her breath caught in her throat. Even now this smile didn't totally encompass him. She always had a sense of part of him being closed off, as if he held a jealously guarded secret. "At the least, distraction."

In the span of a very brief time her self-perception was changing drastically. The way she saw herself was beginning to unravel. Perhaps it had begun with her dreams about Simon and her reaction to him tonight, the way she saw herself since she'd discovered Elliott's unfaithfulness, the way Simon portrayed her in relation to her parents. In a very short time frame her world had shifted and changed and left her floundering. Perhaps the last year in New York had just been a warm-up, and the closest she'd come to discovering her true self had been in the last few minutes.

And she and Simon were getting real. She'd had a glimpse of the real Simon when he'd photographed her for Elliott. What would she see in herself now, were he to photograph her again? She didn't want him to retreat again. She didn't want to dream about him tonight. Tonight she wanted the flesh-and-blood man in her bed.

An idea began to gel. He was so much more approachable when he was behind the camera. If she could talk him into photographing her, she also had a fairly good chance of getting him into her bed.

"Simon, would you do something for me?"

"It depends on what it entails." Ah, ever cautious, ever reserved Simon wasn't crawling out on a limb blind.

"I'm more than willing to pay you."

A wicked smile set her heart thundering. "You've definitely caught my attention now."

Something dark and sexy underlay the note of droll amusement in his voice that sent a wave of desire washing through her. Attention was good for starters, but she definitely wanted more.

"Would you photograph me while we're waiting on the lights to come on? Not for Elliott this time but for me?"

"I'M NOT FOR HIRE," HE SAID. Agreeing to photograph Tawny would be a combined act of madness and desperation.

"Oh." Her disappointment wasn't feigned.

Who was he kidding? He might as well get real with himself. Photographing her would be a sweet torture. Making love to her with his camera was a dismal substitute for actually touching and tasting her but far safer. And when it came down to it, he was incapable of denying her anything. He'd give her the moon if it was his to offer.

"But I will do it for free."

She shook her head, freeing a few strands of hair that promptly clung to her cheek. She brushed them back. "No, I insist on paying."

"Trust me. I'm a selfish bastard. You're much less likely to cry in front of a camera. It isn't gratis as much as self-preservation."

"I only cry when I'm really angry, so you're safe unless you make me mad." She smiled. "I'm beginning to think you're not a selfish bastard at all but that's the image you like to project." She narrowed her eyes at him. "Then we'll barter. I'll plan a party for you one day."

"Absolutely." Right. He had one friend. Elliott.

And he wasn't feeling like throwing a party for him at the moment.

"Or I could set something up more private, for you and your lady if you decided to approach her," she said, as if she'd read his mind.

"You did offer to help me with my sad love life, didn't you?"

"I could set up something very nice and romantic. You really should approach her. You've got so much to offer a woman."

"I've already agreed to photograph you. Blatant lies aren't necessary," Simon said. He laughed to cover his pounding heart.

Tawny smiled and caught him totally off guard when she tossed a small pillow at him and it bounced off of his chest.

"Maybe you need a little dose of your own hard-line truth. Whoever this wonder woman is would be damn lucky to have you. I think you're hiding a very nice guy behind your aloofness. You're smart, occasionally very funny, talented, sexy and I give you high marks in the kissing department."

He didn't know what the hell to say. "Okay."

"At least think about it," she said. "Decide what kind of evening you'd like to have with your own true love. I bet if you ask her, she'll say yes, and I can take care of the rest."

She faced him from the other end of the couch like a luscious piece of fruit just out of reach. Well, unfortunately, closer to his reach than was comfortable. And he didn't have to think about it too hard. He'd want it similar to this. Candlelight. A bottle of wine. Her. Him. Soft, seductive music. He'd sit in a chair and she'd stand just out of reach and slowly peel her clothes off until she was splendidly naked. She'd come closer, close enough for him to touch the velvet of her skin, cup the fullness of her breasts, cull the dew of her desire, inhale the scent of her skin and arousal.... He jerked himself back from the precipice of lust he'd almost plunged over headfirst. "I promise I'll think about it."

"Just let me know when."

"Sure." He levered himself off the couch and crossed to his equipment stored by her door. "Now that we have an agreement, what's your favorite room? Your favorite place? Where do you spend most of your time?"

He pulled out his camera and began setting up the lens. He relaxed into the rote task, pleased to focus on something tangible, something other than his feelings for Tawny.

She hesitated. "The couch is my favorite spot."

He wasn't buying it. She'd thought about it too long for him to believe her.

He looked at her across the candlelit room. She sat perched on her knees, bracing her arms on the sofa back, watching him.

"Come on, Tawny. What happened to honesty in

the dark and all that? Let's try this again. What's your favorite place in your flat?"

Her chin rose a notch. Ah, that was his girl. "The tub. It's an old claw-foot. Great for soaking."

Click. Instant photo in his head. Her, hair piled atop her head, steam rising, skin glistening. He swallowed.

"What's your next favorite place?" No way she missed the hoarseness in his voice, but bloody hell, he was only human.

"The bedroom." Only marginally safer than the bathroom, with her big sleigh bed, but at least naked wasn't a given. "And my least favorite room is the kitchen. I don't like to cook and neither the kitchen nor this room has windows. They feel claustrophobic."

"Then let's photograph you in the bedroom." He strove for a professional tone. She'd hit on the perfect solution to his problem. Photographing her, he became a professional engaged in a shoot instead of Simon Thackeray besotted with Tawny Edwards.

"I definitely want to change clothes. I'm hot and sticky."

"Fine. Take your time. I'll finish setting up my equipment."

"It won't take me long." She picked up a candle and hesitated. "Would you, uh, mind just walking me to the bedroom until I light the candles?" That's right, he'd blown them out earlier. "I hate walking into a dark room."

She had major issues with the dark. But then

again, he had major issues with getting too close in relationships. He knew that. Particularly after one of his girlfriends had flung the accusation at him on her way out the door. Everyone had their own neuroses to bear. "Sure. I'll lead the way so you don't have to walk into the dark room."

"Thank you, Simon."

Her soft voice with it's honeyed Southern drawl slid beneath his skin. Ridiculous, really, that she looked at him as if he'd just agreed to slay dragons on her behalf. Even more ridiculous how good it made him feel.

"You're welcome, Tawny."

A fat candle in hand, he led the way, aware of her close behind him. Unfortunately for him, he now knew how delicious her mouth tasted, how her curves fit against his body as if she'd been tailor-made for him. Just before he reached her room, she placed her hand lightly on his back. Her touch hummed through him.

"Wait a minute. Let's stop by the bathroom. A nice cold washcloth would be heavenly right now. I bet you could use one, too."

How about a nice icy shower? But he'd get by with a cool cloth. "Sure."

He stepped through the dark doorway to his left, the candle illuminating a rectangular room with a small, high window. A claw-foot tub with a circular shower curtain pushed to one side sat beneath the window. The mirror over the sink reflected his light and brightened the bathroom.

Simon sucked in a deep breath as her hip and breast brushed his side, her fingers slid along his back as she squeezed past him in the confines.

"Sorry," she muttered.

"No problem."

She placed her votive on a small shelf next to the sink. Thick, fluffy towels and washcloths sat neatly folded in an open cabinet. She plucked two cloths from the stack and held them under the cold-water tap.

Simon waited beside the sink, next to the door. She squeezed excess water from the cloth and passed one to him.

He ran it over his heated face and watched Tawny do the same. She slid the cloth over her neck, rolling her head to one side and then the other. A half moan, half sigh escaped her. "How good does this feel?" she asked, her voice low, husky, intimate.

"It's somewhere past good." Icy droplets trickled down his throat, raising gooseflesh. It wouldn't surprise him to hear the water sizzle on his skin. She definitely had him hot and bothered. The cloth might be cooling him down, but she was heating him right back up.

"Here. Let me wet it again." She took his cloth and held it under the cold faucet. She held it out to him dripping wet.

Simon set his candle on the widest portion of the sink and took the cloth from her, his fingers brushing hers in the exchange. The brief contact fired through him.

"Have you ever been this hot before?" she asked. "If I spontaneously combust, douse me with water to put out the flames."

Simon had no idea where it came from, but he ran with his impulse. "Like this?" he asked. He stepped closer and squeezed the cloth, cascading water over her shoulder.

She gasped, whether at the shock of the cool water or at his audacity or perhaps both, and then laughed. "Oh, you…"

"Or like this?" He sent another round of droplets skittering down her back, bared by her top.

"Maybe more like this." She reached up and squeezed her cloth at the base of this throat, sending a cool stream down the front of his T-shirt.

He laughed and retaliated. She shrieked and didn't bother with the washcloth, cupping her hands beneath the water and tossing it his way. Within seconds they were both drenched. One of them, their aim so bad, doused the big candle. It sputtered out and ended their water play. Only the small votive flickered, plunging them into intimacy.

"Oops," Tawny said. "That was fun."

Her hair hung drunkenly from its clip. Water sparkled against her skin. The cold water had her nipples standing at full attention against the wet material of her shirt. Simon swallowed hard and looked her in the eyes. *Just don't look back down.*

He cleared his throat. "It was fun."

He had no idea he could be so playful. Water fights had never happened in his house. Hell, fun hadn't happened in his house. His parents had taken their jobs and life very seriously. They still did.

She grabbed a towel off of the stack and he reached for it. She bypassed his hand and instead began to rub his wet hair herself.

"I can do that myself," he said.

"I know." She gentled the towel along his jaw, slid the thick, soft cotton down the column of his throat. "But there, I've taken care of it."

She took a step back and, using the same towel, blotted her face. Simon held out his hand and she gave the towel over to him.

"I can do this myself," she said, echoing his earlier declaration.

"I know." He eased the towel over the length of her neck, across the delicate line of her collarbone, into the valley created by her breasts. Simon made sure only the cotton cloth touched her skin. He moved behind her and slowly, carefully dried her shoulders and the expanse of sweet skin along her spine. He knelt on one knee and drew the towel along her thighs, the backs of her knees, her calves.

"Turn around for me."

She pivoted slowly and he once again slid the towel the length of her legs, the material whispering over her skin.

He stood and silently handed her the towel.

"Thank you," she said.

"No problem."

At least there wouldn't be as soon as they got out of this confined space where she smelled too good, looked too good, felt too good. He picked up the candle she'd carried in. The sooner he got her to her room and put his camera between them, the better off they'd both be.

6

SHE WAS IN DEEP DOO-DOO. Something had just happened there in the bathroom, without even a kiss or an overt touch. She'd gone from mere lust to infatuation. Every inch of her knew that it was no longer a matter of *if* they wound up in her bed together tonight but *when*. He couldn't possibly touch her with such tenderness and not want her. And while part of her was keyed up in anticipation, the knowledge also put her somewhat at ease.

Simon lit the last of the candles in her bedroom.

"I have a couple of T-shirts that are big on me. They'd probably be tight on you, but at least they wouldn't be wet." She fished out a shirt she occasionally slept in because it was two sizes too big. "How about this?"

"Thanks."

"I'll just hold on to it until you get out of that wet one." She knew what she wanted and she was going for it. *Him.*

"Were you planning to watch?"

"Unless you object. A girl's got to get her thrills where she can."

"I'm not sure that I qualify as a thrill."

"I'm certain you do."

Simon tugged his T-shirt loose from his jeans and peeled it up and off his body. Sweet mercy, the man had a body to die for. Broad-shouldered, lean-hipped and nicely trim in between. She felt like Goldilocks who'd just discovered the perfect male. Oh my, that one had been too big and hairy. And oops, that one was too hairless and skinny. But, oh baby, this one was *just* right. And however cliché it was, she found it incredibly sexy the way that dark hair trailed past his navel and disappeared below the waistband of those jeans.

"You, Simon Thackeray, were built to thrill. I'm very…thrilled."

He grinned. Not the arrogant smirk of an overinflated ego but that of a man pleased to be appreciated.

"You want to toss me that shirt you're holding on to?" he said.

She sighed audibly. "I will if I absolutely have to. Don't feel compelled to get dressed on my account." Nonetheless, she tossed it to him.

He caught it single-handedly and sobered. "Are you flirting with me, Tawny?"

"Yes, Simon, I am. Shamelessly."

"Do you think that's a good idea?"

"No. Not really. I think it's probably a very bad

idea, but I'm certainly enjoying it. How about you?" she said.

"Am I enjoying it or do I think it's a good idea?"

"Both."

"I have to go with you on both counts. I'm enjoying it and I'm sure it's a bad idea." He pulled the shirt over his head, hiding that yummy physique.

Spoilsport.

But not to worry, she planned to get it back off of him soon enough.

THERE WAS SOMETHING VERY intimate about being in her candlelit bedroom, knowing she was about to undress. "Hold on a minute. Don't move. I'll be right back."

He sprinted back to the den, snagged his camera and was back in her bedroom within a minute. "I want to capture the moment, the anticipation, the preparation, not just the finished product." Hell, maybe it wasn't a good idea. In fact, he was damn near certain it was a bad idea. But no worse than being here now. And photographing her was safer than kissing her.

When he shot, he became one with the camera. He could be himself behind the lens.

"You want to photograph me changing clothes?"

"Not while you're actually changing but while you're getting ready. Plus it gets you used to being in front of the camera. Just forget I'm here."

She looked across the room, her eyes holding his.

It was a look, one breath away from smoldering, that acknowledged him as a man she'd kissed earlier. "I can't do that."

"Can you forget the camera's here?" He was proud of his steady tone. He didn't feel steady.

"I think so."

He fired off a couple of shots, just to get her used to it. She smiled, self-conscious and awkward. "Just relax," he reminded her. If he could keep her talking, a stream of distracting chatter, she'd also relax. "Do you have your hair up because it's cooler that way?"

"Yes. But it's so hot now, I don't think it's going to matter. And I should do something with it anyway." She turned her back to him and pulled the barrette out and let her hair tumble past her shoulders. His shutter whirred. She shook her head and pushed her fingers through it. He shot again. She looked at him in the mirror, a beguiling mixture of longing and uncertainty, and his heart pounded. Was there anything more enchanting, more intimate, than a woman taking her hair down?

"Better?" she asked.

Click. "Perfect. Keep doing what you're doing."

She raised her arms and reached beneath the fall of her hair. "Beautiful. Beautiful delineation of your neck, shoulders and arms. A study in perfection. A work of art."

"You don't have to say those things, you know."

"I know. But it's true." And it would be so much

better without the interfering lines of her halter top. "Keep your back to me and take your top off," he said, automatically instructing her in what would give the best shot of her back.

"Is that how you get women to undress for you? A few complimentary phrases?" She glanced over her shoulder, laughing, teasing but with a sexy glint in her eyes.

"You're on to me." His responding laugh was rusty. As a rule, he didn't laugh a lot. "No naughty pictures. I just want to capture the line of your back without the top. Move away from the mirror, keep your back to me, take it off and lift your hair that same way. Wait a second. Here. Stand here." He moved her away from the mirror and positioned the tall triple-wick candle—the one she'd earlier said could go all night—until the light illuminated her back. "Just a bit more to the right."

From habit, he lightly touched her, to direct her where he wanted her to go. He'd touched beautiful women wearing far less than Tawny hundreds of times, but it was as if he'd never touched anyone before. And he hadn't. Not like this. Longing swept him, threatened his composure. He felt her indrawn breath, the sudden rigid line of her once-supple back.

He dropped his hand and backed away from her, gripping his camera like a lifeline. "You don't have to take off your top if you don't want to." That steady tone he'd prided himself on earlier was long gone.

"I want to take it off."

She reached beneath her hair and unhooked the top, and he watched the sides fall away and to the front. She lowered her arms and reached to the front. It was a wrap halter and tied in the front—beneath her left breast, he'd noticed. The material bisecting the elegant lines and curves of her back fell away.

"Brilliant. Truly stunning." He fired away. These would be incredible. "Lots of women with beautiful faces aren't lovely from this angle. Lift your hair once again. The way you did before."

She followed his instructions. He'd never gotten emotionally caught up in what he was photographing. It was art and it was his art and in many ways it was an extension of himself, but there was also still an engagement that wasn't personal, that didn't tie his emotions into it. But this was vastly different.

She turned slightly to her right, just enough to reveal the hint of roundness of her breast, the slight sag that meant they were real and not bought in a surgeon's office.

She dropped her arms and turned to face him, her silken curls curtaining the slope of her breasts and nipples, but the soft roundness of the bottom half revealed. Despite the fact she'd turned to face him, there was something more. A subtle shift in her body language, as if she'd discovered something, resolved something.

"Simon, do you have any idea why I've had doubts about me and Elliott?"

It had been one of those remarks he should've taken more note of but had been lost in the higher drama of the moment. He thought it through now. Elliott's turnabout in his sexual orientation had obviously surprised her, so that wasn't it. She didn't appear to have any ambiguity concerning her own. Which meant she'd been seeing someone else or had at the least met someone else. Rancor filled him. He didn't want to hear her confess to yet another attraction. Or perhaps that was exactly what he needed to hear to excise her from his heart, his psyche, his emotions. "My first guess is that you've found someone else, as well."

"Not exactly." Pathetic how glad he was to hear that. "Not the way you mean anyway. I've developed an interest in someone else, even though it hasn't gone any further. Well, sort of."

She had his attention now. Who was he kidding? She always had his attention. She'd owned it from the first time he'd spotted her across the room. "Why don't you explain?"

"I promised you earlier I wouldn't fling myself at you again. And I'm not. But it's time to be honest and I think you should know. It was you, Simon."

She could probably hear his heart pounding from across the room. Tawny had doubted her relationship with Elliott because of *him?* He didn't trust her words. Couldn't trust her words. What would possibly attract her to him over Elliott?

"Don't, Tawny. Don't go there. Elliott might've behaved badly, but I'm not a particularly nice guy and I don't want to be thrust into the role of payback pawn because Elliott's wounded your pride or broken your heart."

She jerked her head back, anger and hurt flashing in her eyes, caught up in the exchange and seemingly unaware that one plump, ripe nipple now peered through her hair. But he was aware enough for both of them. Hell, he was aware enough for an army.

"You think I'm making this up to get back at Elliott?"

"You're not trying to seduce me?"

"I'm trying to be honest, you thickheaded, arrogant, cold-blooded, sarcastic jackass, and you are really…pissing me off."

"Well, I can see, given that glowing description, why I'd be the man to give you second thoughts about marrying Elliott. Perhaps you felt the need to break it off based on the poor company he keeps."

She'd said she was pissed off earlier. She was bloody, wanking angry now.

"Here's the truth, Simon Thackeray, if you can handle it. I'll be damned if I know why, but I've started having dreams about you. About us. They began after we spent the day together for the photo shoot."

"What kind of dreams?" God, he could barely breathe.

"Sexual dreams. Explicit."

"They're just dreams, Tawny."

"I'm well aware of that, Simon. But those dreams, *you*, were beginning to take a toll on my relationship with Elliott."

Instead of gaining clarity, things were growing murkier and more tangled. It had almost been easier when she and Elliott belonged to one another. She'd been off-limits to Simon and his role had been clearly defined. "Why would you let a few dreams interfere with a real relationship?"

"It wasn't a choice and it wasn't just a few dreams. It was almost every night. At first I didn't want to go to sleep, because I didn't want to dream about making love to you." Heat surged through him. She looked down and studied her nails. "And now it's gotten to the point that being asleep is the best part of my day." She looked back up. "And I've felt guilty as hell with Elliott because it felt wrong to do the things with you that I was doing while I was engaged to him." Her gaze captured his. "And doubly wrong because what we had in my dreams was so much better than what Elliott and I had in reality."

Her words seduced him, fired along his nerve endings, tightened his body as surely as if she'd trailed her hands over him. "Maybe you won't have any more of those dreams."

She shook her head. "This afternoon I was napping when Elliott called. I was dreaming and just about to come. With you." And he wasn't so sure that if she went into enough detail he wouldn't come. She had him hard and throbbing. "I've felt like the biggest whore east of the Mississippi. Do you know the first thing that came to mind when he said you both wanted to come over this evening?"

Obviously her mind was an utter mystery to him since he had no clue she'd been having what sounded like very intense sex with him. "No clue."

"Ménage à trois. That's how depraved you've made me. I am trying to seduce you. Not to get back at Elliott. I need the reality of your touch to exorcise those dreams. Because as it stands now, I'm afraid you've ruined me for any other man."

WHEN SHE WAS SEVEN, frustrated by her lack of progress in her swimming classes, without really thinking it through, she'd sucked in a deep breath and jumped in over her head. And from that day forward her philosophy had taken shape: she'd swim or die trying. Obviously she'd swum.

And she'd just plunged in far out of her depth with Simon. But it was true. She feared he'd ruined her for any other man. And if she could offer him an outlet for his unrequited love, then why not?

Simon advanced toward her, beginning to click off picture after picture.

"Tawny, I'm sure that I haven't ruined you for other men, as you'll find when you get back in-to…circulation."

Circulation. Another man's bed was what he meant. And obviously he had no intention of or interest in being that man. Yet another dose of humiliation washed over her.

Why hadn't she simply kept her mouth shut? Why had she let a few erotic dreams and one helluva live kiss convince her she and Simon had chemistry?

Obviously all the chemistry was in her head—as in chemical imbalance. Obviously he was willing to photograph her. Obviously he'd been offering her comfort earlier and she'd misread the situation. And now obviously she needed to put some freaking clothes on and try to maintain a few shreds of dignity until the power was restored and Simon was out her door. And out of her life.

"You're right. A little circulation will take care of that for me." She aimed for light and laughing, but it came out stiff and abrupt. She was precariously close to total humiliation. "Let me put some clothes back on."

She headed for her closet. Maybe she could spend an hour or so in there—except it was dark. She'd never let herself get caught without a flashlight ever again.

"Tawny—"

Simon touched her bare shoulder. She froze outside while heat filled her on the inside. "Simon, please don't touch me."

"That's not what you said a moment ago."

She ached for him. And what was the small matter of pride? She'd already humiliated herself. "You know what I mean. I'm not sure that I can stand for you to touch me and not take it any further. And since you're not interested in going there, it's best if you simply don't touch me at all."

His hand remained on her shoulder. Yearning like nothing she'd ever known before filled her. She wanted him with a desperation that bordered on obsession.

"I didn't say I wasn't interested." His fingers moved against her bare skin in a featherlight caress. "I just don't want you to regret this tomorrow."

Moving in slow motion, she turned to face him. "I'm not looking for forever. I want you for tonight. I know you're in love with someone else. Let me be her for you tonight."

"You would sleep with me, knowing I may very well pretend you're someone else?"

She lifted her chin a notch. "Yes. You turn me on that much." She wasn't exactly shy and retiring to begin with, but there was a fantastic quality to being in her candlelit bedroom with Simon. She said things she would never have been bold enough to say in the harsh light of day. "I'll take whatever you're offering, except I don't particularly want to be a pity lay."

"You won't be standing in for anyone. This is about me and you. I wouldn't insult you by pretending you were anyone other than who you are." He tilted her head back with one finger beneath her chin and stared hard into her eyes. There wasn't a shred of pity in his eyes. They burned with a heat and a leashed passion for her. "And I don't want to be a revenge lay."

"Never," she said, winding her arms around his neck, feeling the corded tension of his body, already wet for him, hungering for his touch. "This isn't payback."

She wanted to quench this desire for Simon that consumed her and she wanted him to make her feel like a desirable woman. Right or wrong, she needed a little sexual validation.

He brushed his thumb over her cheekbone. "Is this really what you want, Tawny? Are you certain you want me? Because stopping will be torture once I touch you, taste you."

She leaned into him, unerringly fitting her hips to his. His cock was rock-hard against her mound, offering instant validation and stimulation. Her panties were drenched and her body was on fire. She rubbed her bare breasts against his shirt, delighting in the soft cotton against her aroused nipples. She breathed in his male scent and nuzzled his jaw. His breath quickened.

"Yes, I'm absolutely certain I want you. And I don't want you to stop. I want you naked on top of me—" she nibbled at his earlobe "—beneath me—" she teased the tip of her tongue along the rim "—beside me—" he shuddered against her "—behind me—" want thickened her voice and strummed through her body "—but most of all inside me."

HER WORDS AND HER TOUCH destroyed every defense he'd erected. He stood to lose the only friend he'd ever really had, Elliott, by sleeping with Tawny. But he'd trade his friendship and essentially his sense of honor, all of his tomorrows, for one night with her, to hold her, touch her, make love to her. And if he was a lesser man for this decision, he had the rest of his life to deal with it. Perhaps he'd dine on the bitter fruit of regret with tomorrow's dawn, but for tonight she was his.

He slid his camera to the floor, dropping the strap. "Tawny…"

He cradled her head in his hands. Without rushing, he kissed her gently, thoroughly, an unspoken promise that for the night, they belonged to each other. He told her in a kiss all the things that he couldn't or wouldn't say aloud—how much he wanted her, how beautiful he found her both inside and out, that among women she alone was the most desirable, that for years he'd carried the Hades analogy in his head and she had become his Persephone, but after tonight he'd release her, after offering and taking solace in her.

She returned his kiss, melded into him, connected with his soul.

The kiss heated, shifted to a higher intensity as she slid her hands beneath his shirt, greedily stroking his bare skin. Her touch ignited him. He reached between them and cupped her breasts in his hands, plying his thumbs against her nipples. She felt so good. Tawny pressed against him and moaned into his open mouth, and Simon was lost, gone. He sank onto the edge of the bed, pulling her down with him, between his thighs.

She followed, settling between his legs.

"It seems as if I've waited forever to touch you," she said. She pressed a kiss to the underside of his jaw while she explored his chest with her hands, bold strokes that fanned the fire inside him hotter and higher.

She reached for his belt and his jeans.

"Wait a sec. Let me take off my boots," Simon said. Tawny stood. He bent down and unlaced his boots—infinitely better than winding up with his trousers around his ankles. Tawny stripped out of her shorts and skimpy panties, dropping them on the floor in front of him. He pulled off the second Doc Martens and looked up.

He was glad he was sitting for his first view of her gloriously, spectacularly naked. She was every inch rounded woman, from shapely legs, to curved hips, to a small waist and full breasts. And obviously a proponent of the Brazilian wax.

Desire slammed him, tightened his balls. "You're so beautiful, you take my breath."

She smiled and there was a shyness about it that touched him. She slid onto the bed behind him and laughed softly, her breath warm against his bare shoulder. She smoothed her hands over his shoulders and nuzzled his neck, her breasts pressed against his back. Her touch sizzled along his nerve endings.

"I'm glad I'm not sending you running out the door," she said.

"Not a chance." He undressed and she pulled him back down onto the bed with her.

He rolled over and trapped her beneath him, his arms on either side of her shoulders. Her eyes darkened and she parted her lips, wetting the fullness of her lower lip with the tip of her tongue.

"The only thing that could possibly send me running is—" he lowered his head and tasted the sweetness of her neck, her shoulder "—if you tell me you've changed your mind."

"No. That…won't…happen." She arched her back, raising herself, inviting his kisses. Bathed in candlelight, her skin gleamed like a rare pearl. He licked the hollow of her throat and chased her shudder with his own. Her scent, the slight saltiness of her skin, the taste of her. He wanted to make love to her all night, learn every inch of her with his mouth, his tongue, his hands. But he'd wanted her so long, he didn't think he could wait much longer this first time around. He circled one plump nipple with his tongue. She moaned deep in her throat.

"Simon…" Tawny said in an agonized tone.

He flicked the other one with the tip of his tongue

and then moved back to the first one—tasting her, tormenting them both.

They were both slick with sweat and her skin slid against his, her thigh cushioning the length of his erection.

She rolled him onto his back and kissed him as if she couldn't get enough. Her tongue dueled with his. Her hands explored him, almost frantic, and she made small whimpering noises in the back of her throat, leaving him hotter and harder. She seemed to want him as much as he wanted her. She rolled to her side again, pulling him with her, reaching behind her without taking her mouth from his. Simon broke the kiss.

"What are you doing?" he asked.

"Reaching for a condom."

He was such a dolt, he'd forgotten all about protection. That had never happened. He'd always been careful. That she kept a stock on hand wasn't particularly surprising, considering her battery-powered arsenal.

She looked at him, her eyes luminous, hot. "I'm so afraid this is another dream," she said. "I don't want to wake up. Because if I do, I'm going to be righteously pissed."

Simon laughed. She had the most unorthodox way of flattering him, but he was immeasurably flattered that she didn't want to wake up if she was dreaming.

"No. We're not dreaming," he said, stroking his hand down her back, over the lush curve of her bum. Reality had never been so sweet.

She held a condom aloft in triumph. "Strawberry flavored." She tore into the package. "Mind if I do the honors?"

"Please. Feel free to," he said.

"My pleasure is—" she stroked the condom over him, her hand warm, with just the right amount of pressure, and he closed his eyes in a moment of *ahhhh* "—your pleasure."

So far she'd only just touched him. She tightened her hand and stroked again. His eyes flew open.

"Unless you want the shortest foreplay in the history of man, you don't need to do that again," he said, his hoarseness reflecting the strain of not coming.

"I'm ready if you're ready. I've had weeks of dreaming about you. That's been plenty of foreplay."

Simon knew a moment of performance anxiety. What if the real him didn't measure up to the dream lover he'd been for her? And the curious, mystical, magical woman that she was, she obviously saw it in his face.

"Don't even go there." She leaned over him and scattered kisses over his chest, laving his male nipples, down his belly. She lapped at his rigid length and took him into her warm, eager mouth. Simon called on every ounce of his self-control not to blast off as she fondled him with her mouth. She released him and he managed to breathe again. Her hair brushed against his belly, the strands teasing against his skin. "Actually tasting you, touching you, smelling you, is so much better than it ever was in my dreams," she said, her tone as hot as the passion glittering in her eyes.

She fell to her back, spread her legs, and said with a sweet smile, "Now are you going to fuck me or do I have to beg first?"

It sent him totally over the edge when she said that. If he was any hotter, he'd melt.

He positioned himself between her legs and nudged at her with his sheathed tip. "No begging necessary."

Simon slid into her slowly, totally captured by the expression on her face, heat and pleasure suffusing her features. She felt so good, so right, and as he slid into her inch by inch, she gripped him, as if welcoming him home.

She wrapped her legs around him and hooked her feet behind his thighs. She lunged up to meet him. A few quick thrusts and they'd both be there. He drew a deep, shuddering breath and deliberately slowed them down. They weren't going for a distance record—they were both wound too tight, they didn't have a prayer of making it far—but he pulled back slowly until he was almost out of her and then treated them both to a slow reentry. Tawny gasped aloud and pushed into him, sending him plunging.

"You are deliciously wicked, Simon Thackeray."

Her honeyed Southern drawl wrapping around his name at the same time her honeyed channel wrapped around his cock nearly undid him. It was as if she'd woven some magic around them, bound them together in a union that went beyond the physical. As if she'd opened up a part of herself and invited him into the warmth and light that was more than skin-deep with her.

She was so open, so giving, and he wanted to give in return. He offered as much of himself as he could. He rode her harder and faster. Her head whipped back and forth on the bed, her hands fisted in the comforter and she urged him on until they were both caught up in the throes of a screaming orgasm—literally.

His Tawny was no wilting flower. She was bold and beautiful, and if he'd ever had a moment's hesitation that he might be standing in for Elliott, she dispelled that particular notion as she panted his name over and over as she shuddered beneath him.

Had she screamed Elliott's name the same way? Had she thrashed beneath him and arched into him as if she'd die without his touch? He absolutely didn't need to go there, yet he absolutely couldn't help himself.

She lay so still beneath him, her eyes closed, that if she hadn't been breathing heavily he might've thought her asleep. A slow smile bloomed on her generous mouth and she opened her eyes.

"That was…incredible…so much better than I ever dreamed it."

A strange sensation filled him. It took a moment

for Simon to recognize it was contentment—utter bloody contentment. He answered her smile with one of his own. He didn't think he could not smile at this point, it was a totally involuntary reaction.

"Absolutely." And then because he wanted to share what he felt but had no clue how to say it, he kissed her, slowly, tenderly, an aftermath of passion.

He traced the curve of her side, his fingers molding against the softness of her skin. He had been painfully honest earlier—now that he was touching her he wasn't sure he could stop. Intellectually he knew skin was skin, an amalgamation of tissue and nerves and cells, but she felt like no other woman beneath his fingertips. He was so absolutely in love with her, loved her so completely, his whole being ached with it.

He lifted his head and looked at her. He dared so much more in the dark. Hiding in the shadows cast by the candlelight, he drank her in. Her hair spread in disarray across the bed, her eyes dark and mysterious, her lips swollen from his kisses, her body relaxed from his lovemaking. Without thought, he ran his fingers along the delicate line of her jaw, breathed in her fragrance. She captured his hand in hers, brought his fingers to her lips and feathered the lightest caress across them.

"Simon…" She hesitated.

"Yes?"

"I don't want to make you uncomfortable—" she glanced away "—but I…I'm not sure how to say this."

His heart, not fully recovered from their sexual calisthenics, began to pound again. "Just say it."

He was too raw and open to quell the surge of hope that she might profess newfound feelings for him.

"I…we…oh, this is so awkward…."

He could barely breathe. Had she discovered, in the aftermath of making love—and that's what it'd been for him—deeper feelings for him?

"What, luv?" Endearments had never been a part of his vocabulary. They'd never been given as a child and he'd never cultivated them as an adult, but this one rolled off his tongue.

"I'm sweaty and sticky and I'm afraid I, well, stink. I need a shower."

Righto. He laughed at himself, at how off the mark he'd been. His brain must've still been centered in his willy. God knows, he knew he wasn't the most lovable guy on the planet. Not even his parents had ever loved him. That wasn't exactly the heartfelt declaration he'd built himself up for but she was right—they were both slick with sweat and although he might be a fool, he wasn't fool enough to turn down an opportunity tonight. "Need a back washer?"

7

"COME ON IN. THE WATER'S fine," Tawny said. She leaned back, welcoming the kiss of cool, smooth porcelain against her back.

"Give me a second." He strode out of the bathroom.

They might be here through force of circumstance, but it was very romantic with candles bathing the room in soft light and contrasting shadows. She'd placed votives in saucers on the floor around the tub. Nothing quite like being inventive.

The candlelight lent a dreamlike air. But it was more than that. The entire night was surreal. Simon Thackeray was about to climb into a bath with her after they'd just had fantastic sex that had been both tender and explosive. She'd discovered a consideration behind Simon's reserve she'd never anticipated, a quality that had never been part of her dreams yet had engaged her beyond the mere physical.

Simon returned, his camera slung around his neck. He should've looked sort of silly wearing only a camera, but there was nothing remotely silly about Simon naked. Impressive. Sexy. Drool-inducing.

Heat flushed her body, regardless of the tepid water surrounding her. Nice—that was such an insipid word—muscular legs, nice package up front, totally nice ass. Wow.

Click.

She laughed. "Did you just take a picture of me ogling you from the bath?"

"Absolutely. Very sexy."

And there was a bonus to carrying on a conversation with a naked man. When he told you he found something sexy, well, you got visual proof to back up his statement. Simon wasn't lying—it looked as if he found her very sexy indeed.

"I'm not actually naked in the picture, am I?"

He grinned. "No. At this angle and with the water at that level, you can't actually see details—which is something of a shame since you possess very nice details."

"Careful, sir. You'll make me swoon," she teased in an exaggerated Southern drawl. Beneath Simon's sober exterior beat the heart of a flirt, and it was all the more potent because he didn't flirt indiscriminately the way some men did. She'd never seen this flirtatious side of him, even when she and Elliott had double-dated with him. Elliott. She didn't remotely want to dedicate a brain cell to Elliott at this moment.

"What do you think will happen when I get in the tub with you, Tawny?"

He was a devil to tease her in that low, suggest-ive tone.

"Keep talking that way and it'll be your own fault if the water's heated up by the time you get here," she said.

Simon laughed and kept firing off pictures. Taw-ny had lost her self-consciousness in front of the camera. She simply ignored it and flirted with Simon.

"You're blowing your chance at cool and refresh-ing."

"Wet and warm sounds even better," he said.

"Getting warmer by the minute. Why don't you come on over and find out just how wet and hot it is?" She sat up, wrapping her arms around her knees. "Don't forget, you promised me a back wash."

"I plan to fulfill that promise thoroughly in just a minute. That's a great angle. Hold it for me."

At one time she might've been impatient, but she knew Simon would join her sooner or later. She eyed his smooth, firm erection—sooner from the looks of things. Anticipation hummed through her and she smiled her anticipation at him.

"Beautiful…oh, that's brilliant," he said, shooting photo after photo.

"I bet you say that to all the girls," she teased, however a part of her rebelled at being just another photograph in a long line.

"I do say that to all the girls." The bottom dropped out of her stomach. That was *not* what she wanted to hear. He looked around the camera and grinned at her. He appeared young and carefree, which were two words she'd never thought to associate with Simon. Her heart did a funny flip-flop. "But I don't climb into a bath with them afterward."

Rat bastard. "I'm sure it's not for lack of opportunity," she said.

"Thanks…I think." He almost looked embarrassed. "I've had a fair share of invitations."

No stinking kidding. He was gorgeous and sexy. The heat inside her grew hotter still—he wanted to climb in the tub with her, Tawny Edwards, as opposed to Chloe and the other exquisite, thin women he photographed. Of course, there was the matter of his dream woman, the unavailable, but Tawny wouldn't think about that because right now he was naked and here with her. Carpe diem.

"It's time to put the camera down, Simon."

He quirked his brows at her, amusement dancing in his eyes. "Do you think I'm just a puppet to be controlled? Are you always so bossy?"

She was. She knew it. "Only when I want something really bad."

"And I'm really bad?" His wicked sexy grin set her pulse fluttering.

"That's totally a matter of perspective. It's been my experience that you're especially good when you're really bad. And I can promise you I want you that way."

He placed the camera next to the wall. Anticipation notched tighter inside her as he crossed the small area. Once he lost the camera he carried himself with a measure of self-consciousness he hadn't had before. She found it endearing that despite his arrogance, he didn't strut around as if he and his dick were God's gift to womankind.

She'd had all those hot dreams about him, so the great sex was…well, great but no real surprise. But she hadn't anticipated actually liking him. And she did. He was tender and funny and sexy and… He stepped into the tub behind her and shot her train of thought to hell.

He sat down, sliding his legs on either side of her. He wrapped his arms around her, pulling her into the V of his body, as if it had been custom designed just for her. Her back curved against his belly and his chest, her head resting between his shoulder and his neck.

Despite their earlier flirtatious patter, Simon seemed equally content to enjoy the moment. She closed her eyes and absorbed the sensations. The rhythm of his heartbeat echoed against her back, his arms were strong yet tender around her. She'd had a boyfriend once who, when he'd put his arms around her, it had been like being locked in a vise grip. Eddie could take a lesson or two from Simon, who definitely knew how to hold a woman. He smelled enticingly of sex, sweat and his own scent.

Candlelight danced across the walls and ceiling.

She was living one of those perfect, wildly romantic moments portrayed in movies and glossy magazines. She sighed, happy to be here, in this moment, now.

"Comfy?" he asked.

"Mmm. Very. You make a nice bath pillow."

"Great. Now I've gone from puppet to pillow," he groused.

Tawny smiled and pressed a kiss to his bicep. "But you're a very sexy bath pillow." Never had her dreams been this good. She was at the head of the line when it came to appreciating great sex, but there was also much to recommend this lazy, comfortable teasing with an undercurrent of anticipation.

He nuzzled his lips against her hair and Tawny could have sworn warm butter replaced all the bones in her body. She melted against him.

"There's a place near my grandparents' farm that my cousin Reg and I used to go to. There's a pool in the middle of the woods with a small waterfall. The pool's shallow enough that the sun heats the water. You can stretch out and sun on this huge flat rock. The water's clear and the air's sweet. When we were young, we thought fairies lived there."

He'd painted such a picture, she could see the place. She also saw a young, intense Simon looking for fairies. A warmth that had nothing to do with physical desire filled her. She knew from the amount of time she'd spent with him and through the things Elliott had divulged about Simon that he was an intensely private man. Maybe it was just the craziness of the night or the unusual circumstances, but she was certain he'd just shared a part of himself few had been privy to before her. And the notion of a young, romantic boy who believed in fairies didn't surprise her nearly as much as it would have at one time. He was a complex, complicated man. She'd wanted him in her bed, but now she found she wanted to know more about the man himself.

"It sounds lovely."

"It is. You'd like it."

"I'm sure I would." *Take me there.* The idea sneak-attacked her. "Do you go to England often?"

"I used to go once a year in the summer. Now I get over a couple of times a year. My father's parents died several years ago. My mother's parents still live in Devon. They're amazing. They're in their mid-eighties and they still keep a small farm going."

"You're close to them?" She'd only ever known her paternal grandparents, and they were even more starched and conservative than her father.

"As close as you can be with an ocean separating you. I spent glorious summers there when I was growing up." She heard his smile.

"Do you go with your parents?"

"No." The sudden chill in his tone was a stark contrast to his earlier warmth. His body tensed against her back, his arms tightened slightly. She intensely disliked Simon's parents even though she'd never met them. By virtue of how little he said, she had a pretty clear picture of two self-absorbed, self-important people who didn't make time for their son. She might be the odd man out in her family, but she still knew they loved her even though they often disapproved of her.

"I can't imagine you on a farm." She deliberately interjected a light, teasing note.

"I'll have you know I'm quite proficient at gathering eggs and milking a cow."

"No way. *That* I'd like to see." Despite her teasing, it was true. She'd like to see Simon unplugged. "Did you have a girlfriend there?"

"No."

"What's wrong with the girls in England? I can't believe you didn't have a girlfriend."

"Devon's not exactly a metropolis like New York or London."

"Are you telling me the countryside was totally devoid of young women? You never wowed a milkmaid one farm over with your egg-gathering technique?"

Simon chuckled, but it sounded forced. "There was one girl...her father was the vicar."

Sometimes he wasn't the most forthcoming with info. Fortunately Tawny didn't mind asking questions. "How British...the vicar's daughter. And her name was...?"

"Jillian. Jillian Carruthers."

"And what ever happened to Jillian Carruthers? Or do you still see her when you go to England?"

"I do still see Jillian, almost every trip."

"Oh." Oh. Crud. Suddenly her teasing and Jillian weren't quite so funny. In fact, Tawny felt sort of nauseous.

"She married my cousin Reg. They're expecting twins this fall."

"Oh." Surely that hadn't been pleasant to have his love interest marry his cousin. Was Jillian his unattainable woman? Yet, Simon had said his unattainable woman wasn't married. Tawny knew she was an evil bitch to feel so relieved Jillian was safely out of the picture. "Is it awkward when you see them?"

"Not at all. That was a long time ago."

She stroked her thumb over his arm, feeling the play of muscle beneath skin. "Did you ever tell her how you felt?"

"I did, in fact. But by the end of the summer, she decided I wasn't her cup of tea. She and Reg became an item and that was that."

Hmm. And there was more there than he was letting on. His tone was light and nonchalant, but she felt the tension in his body. "Were you devastated?"

"Only for a bit. They're well-suited. It worked out that way for a reason. Life has a way of doing that."

She didn't want him to retreat due to a memory of a lost love. She deliberately brought the conversation back to them. "I for one am glad it worked out that way because otherwise I wouldn't be sitting here with you. Jillian has no idea what she's missing." She wriggled, pressing her buttocks against him, a not-so-subtle reminder of where he was, who he was with, and the direction things were headed. "I think you're lots of fun."

"Do you now?" He pressed a kiss to the nape of her neck, seeming to inherently know her most sensitive spot. He laughed softly at her intake of breath and the shiver she had no hope of hiding.

"Yes," she said. His teeth raked lightly against her shoulder and she shuddered at the exquisite sensation. "And I'm particularly fond of that kind of fun."

"I'm just getting started with the fun. I owe you a back wash." He released her and she passed him the soap. "Lean forward a bit."

She folded her arms over her knees and rested her head on them. He stroked his soapy fingers over her shoulders, traced down the line of her backbone and then rubbed small circles over her back. She almost purred, it felt so good. "Ahh. You certainly know how to wash a back."

"Your back has beautiful lines." He curled his fingers along her right side. "This curve. Very graceful."

Oh. The things he did and said—the way he made her feel. What was it about Simon that he unlocked more feelings, more response in her with a single touch than any man ever had with far more than a touch?

"Thank you. And don't even think about stopping and getting your camera."

"I'm not going anywhere." Heat underscored his teasing tone.

The water lapped around her as he gentled his soap-slicked hands up her sides, his fingertips barely brushing the sides of her breasts, to her underarms. My God, she'd never had anyone stroke her underarms, never knew it could feel so good.

She raised her head and uncrossed her arms when he cupped his hands and ran them over her upper arms. He stroked the length of her limbs and she leaned back into him once again, her breasts tingling, tightening in anticipation of where his hands would roam next.

He reached around, beneath her arms, and worked his finger magic across her collarbone, along her chest leading to the slope of her breasts and then the curve of her breasts, along the side, beneath them but never actually touching them or her nipples. Finally he cupped them and she dropped her head back against him, the thud of his heartbeat strong against her shoulder.

"Yes."

"Is this what you wanted?" His breath gusted against her neck. "Is this what you've been waiting for?"

"Yes."

"Me, too," he purred next to her ear while his fingers found her nipples. Warmth rushed between her thighs as he plucked and kneaded and caressed. Judging by the way his cock surged against her back, he enjoyed fondling her breasts as much as she enjoyed his "fun."

He cupped his hands and sluiced water over her front, rinsing off the soap.

"Now your back." She leaned forward and he rinsed. He settled her once again against his chest.

"Feel better?" He traced the shell of her ear with the tip of this tongue.

"Much." He expected her to think coherently…talk…when his tongue and mouth were…ooh.

"I think you can feel even better yet," he said, low and seductive.

She closed her eyes when he kissed her neck. She *loved* having her neck kissed. It tingled through her body all the way to her toes. He could spend hours kissing her neck and she'd be a happy camper.

"I don't know…I'm feeling…ooh…very good."

"We'll see about that," he said and anticipation coursed through her. He ran his hands over the rounded mound of her belly and she tried to suck it in, to flatten it. His warm breath teased against her ear. "Stop, Tawny. Relax. You're built like a woman's supposed to be built. Soft, with curves in all the right places."

Go to the head of the class for that answer, Simon. He was so tuned in to her, seemed to read every nuance of her body language. He trailed his fingers, the lightest of touches, along the tops of her thighs.

"Open your legs for me." His voice was as thick as his erection nudging her from behind and reminded her of her dream that morning. It was a perfect blend of fantasy and reality and left her all the hotter still. She spread her legs and cool water rushed against her slick heat.

Simon reached between her thighs, his arms and hands dark against her pale skin, and parted her with his thumbs. "Oh, luv, I like your bare style."

It had taken two margaritas of Dutch courage to actually work up the nerve to have another human being wax her *there* and it had hurt like hell, but when it was all said and done, once she'd gone bare she was never going back.

She inched her legs farther apart. "Me, too. The better to feel you."

And feel him she did—every screaming, craving nerve ending in her body centered between her legs. He traced her with a finger until he found her clit and brushed against it. She whimpered and pressed against his hand. Okay, maybe her neck wasn't her *most* sensitive spot.

"Easy. Relax. Not so fast. Sit back and enjoy it. Savor it. You liked it when I did that?"

"Yes."

"How about his?" He slid a finger into her and she forced herself not to arch into him, but she did clench her muscles around him.

"Yes."

"You feel so good. You're so much hotter than the water. It's like dipping my finger into warm honey."

His voice, low and sexy, his words, his touch, the feel of his body behind her, his arms around her, the feel of his breath against her skin when he spoke, the faint scrape of his whiskers against her shoulder, the cool water lapping at her hot skin, all centered in her, through her.

He alternated stroking along her slit and sliding a finger, then two fingers, into her, while his thumb worked magic on her clit. He cupped her left breast in his other hand, toying with her nipple, plucking, squeezing.

Tawny gripped the sides of the tub and spread her legs wider, pressing against his hair-roughened legs on either side of her. *Please.* She couldn't stand anything that felt this good much longer, but she also didn't want it to stop.

"Harder. Faster. Yes…yes…like that…oh…" She thrust her hips up to meet his fingers, driving him deeper within her, grinding her clit against the pressure of his thumb.

"That's it, luv. You're so beautiful. I want you to come for me. That's it…" Simon's voice sent her over the edge. She turned her head and bit into his shoulder, suckling him, tasting the warm saltiness of his skin against her tongue as she spasmed with pleasure.

She collapsed against him, quite simply because

she didn't seem to have a bone left in her body. She felt as fluid and formless as the water surrounding her.

Simon pressed a kiss to her hair and wrapped his arms more firmly around her. "Oh, Tawny."

"Mmm," she murmured and rubbed her cheek against his arm, the only response she was capable of at the moment. Slowly she came back together, fully aware of his hard ridge behind her, the taut muscles of his belly and chest, the tension banding his arms.

She slid forward and turned around to face him on her knees. Sexual arousal and need etched his face, glittered in his eyes. With a slow smile she reached for the soap.

"Your turn."

"I CAN'T GET IT UP," TAWNY said, her frustration evident in the way she shoved her hair back off of her brow. "Do you want to try?"

"Sure. I'll have a go at it." God this would be embarrassing if he couldn't get it up for her, but there was no guarantee. He put his weight behind pulling up on the window sash. "These older buildings have been painted so many times, sometimes the window's painted shut." He felt the smallest amount of give. "I think it's coming." Yep. The window gave and opened a few inches. He wrestled it the rest of the way.

"My hero," she said, teasing him with a smile, but

her eyes shone with something that wrapped around his heart.

God, he was hopeless. He felt ten feet tall just because he'd opened the bloody window for her.

"It's no Arctic blast, but it's a bit cooler than in here." The drenching rain had brought little relief from the relentless heat. Steam rose from the pavement below.

"When it rains at home, it's steamy, too. But New York never smells fresh the way Savannah does after a rain," Tawny said on a wistful note. She swept back the comforter and top sheet and settled against the pillows propped against her headboard. "At least the sheets are sort of cool."

She obviously had no intention of sitting in the cloying confines of her den. Suited him fine. He stretched across the end of the bed, a towel around his hips. His damp clothes were draped over the shower rod in the bathroom. She'd had the benefit of fresh clothes and wore a pair of black panties, which were really just plain but very sexy, and a black tank top.

"Do you miss Savannah?" he asked.

"I miss certain things about it. The way it smells after a summer rain. The sound of a horse-drawn carriage on cobblestones. Spanish moss draping trees so old and sprawling they canopy the streets. Have you ever been there?"

"No. I'm not well traveled outside of New York and England."

She traced a lazy pattern on his calf with her toe. He liked the casual way she touched him, as if she needed to and had the right to. "The slower pace might drive you insane, but you'd love the city itself."

They lay in the flickering light, with the sounds of New York drifting in through the window, and she painted a picture for him of her birthplace, of the history and architecture and culture. Whether she knew it or not, her voice slowed, took on more of that honeyed Southern accent that always underlay her words. He imagined the two of them enjoying a horse-drawn carriage ride along cobblestone streets beneath moss-drenched oaks.

"You obviously love it. Why'd you leave?"

"I do love it, and in a way it was hard to go, but not really. I left because I needed to."

"Needed to or wanted to?"

"*Needed* to. I needed to step out of my comfort zone, discover new places, new things, discover myself."

She intrigued him with her mix of gutsiness, attitude, open sensuality and insecurities.

"And have you? Discovered yourself?" he asked.

"I thought I had. Tonight's sort of blown me out of the water. But I think I've finally figured out it's an ongoing process. Every day brings something new and different—some days more than others—like today. I know for certain I'm not the same person I was when I left, and that's a good thing."

How did she feel about today's changes? After this

fiasco with Elliott, would she think about moving back home? She didn't strike Simon as the type to run home to her mother, but he had to ask.

"After this with Elliott, are you thinking about moving back?"

She shook her head and gave him a funny look. Tendrils of loose hair danced across her shoulders. "Not in the foreseeable future. I love Savannah and it'll always be home—I look forward to my visits—but New York has a pretty firm hold on my heart, as well. What about you? Have you ever wanted to live somewhere else?"

Tawny was easy to talk to and the dark didn't hurt either. Simon found himself telling her things he'd never told anyone else, perhaps never truly thought about consciously. "When I was a kid spending my summers in Devon, I wanted to stay there forever. When I got older, I realized it was my grandparents that drew me and not the place itself. Once I moved out on my own, New York felt more like home."

"My parents aren't exactly warm and fuzzy either."

They weren't even touching—well, except for her toe against his calf—but he felt closer to her emotionally than he ever had to anyone, even Elliott. He almost told her he hadn't said that about his parents, but he supposed he had. Indirectly. She had a way of seeing through to him. And as she'd said earlier, what was the point of prevarication.

"But you're warm and outgoing. How did that happen?"

"I'm an anomaly, the *which one of these doesn't belong.*" She laughed and the rueful note tore at his heart.

"I've always been the odd man out, as well." He'd thought it innumerable times. It was liberating to say it.

"What are they like?" she asked.

"My parents?" She nodded. "Clever, engaging, articulate. They're a self-contained unit. They made wonderful cocktail-party guests and lousy parents."

"No brothers or sisters?"

"Nope. Just me." And it had been just him in every respect. They hadn't been a family. Growing up had been such a lonely experience until he and Elliott became friends that he didn't particularly want to revisit it. "What was it like with two sisters?"

He switched the conversation back to her. She looked at him and he knew she was onto him, but she indulged him nonetheless, launching into tales about her siblings.

She was a natural storyteller. He loved the rhythm and cadence of her voice. There was a soothing quality to her speech even when she was regaling him with her childhood escapades.

"You might be the baby of the family, but I'm seeing a pattern here. You're definitely the instigator."

"Hmm. I told you…I'm the one who doesn't quite fit." Drowsiness exaggerated her drawl.

"You sound tired," he said.

"I am. What time is it?"

Simon checked his luminous watch. "Almost midnight."

"It's still early, but I think I'm emotionally exhausted and then too much fun…"

"Get some sleep."

"Mmm. That's a good idea."

They'd had sex twice, but there was such an intimacy to actually sharing a bed with another person, letting your guard down enough to drift into unconsciousness….

"Would you rather have me on the couch?" he asked.

"No. Stay with me." *Don't read more into it than she means.* "It's cooler in here…and I don't want you to go. I changed the sheets this morning, if that was…you know, if you felt funny about… I'm making a mess of this."

"You're not making a mess of anything." He slid up the bed to stretch out beside her. She was one woman in a million—concerned that sleeping on sheets after Elliott would bother him. He ran his finger down the line of her nose and pressed a chaste good-night kiss to her forehead. "Thank you for telling me. Go to sleep and I'll be right here."

She smiled sleepily, hands-down the most beautiful smile he'd ever seen, on or off camera. "Try to sleep, too." She found his leg with her foot.

"I will."

He lay in her bed and listened to the muted sounds from a city that never slept, even in the midst of a blackout, and the soft cadence of her breathing. Without forethought, he lightly stroked her hair away from her face, wanting only to touch her while he still could, unwilling to sleep away his time with her. She uttered a soft satisfied sound.

"Simon?"

"Hmm?"

"I'm glad tonight happened." Imminent sleep slurred her words.

"So am I," he said.

Despite the suffocating heat, she shifted closer to him and—what the hell, they were both sweaty and sticky—he pulled her into his body. Her thigh slid between his and she curled her arm across his chest. She pressed a tender, drowsy kiss to his chest and he quietly fell a little harder, faster, deeper in love with her.

8

"NO! COME BACK!"

Bloody hell! Simon jerked up, momentarily disoriented by the strange bed, candles and a screeching woman. Righto. Tawny. Her bed. Blackout.

"What's the matter?" He jumped to his feet and grabbed Tawny, who shook like a leaf.

"Peaches." She gulped air and motioned to the bedroom window. "He pushed through the screen and went out the window. He's on the ledge." She death-gripped his arm. "He doesn't have any front claws. What if he slips out there?"

She loved that cat. Simon didn't hesitate, didn't think, he just did. He worked the screen loose, tossed it back into the room and stuck his head out the window.

"Can you see him?" Tawny squeezed into the window opening. "Oh, God."

Peaches, now that the deed was done, apparently realized the error of his ways and huddled on the ledge several feet away.

She lowered her voice. "Come on, baby. C'mere,

Peaches. I've got a nice kitty treat waiting for you." Her voice shook.

Peaches yowled in kitty hysteria but didn't budge. Brilliant. If the people in the next apartment opened their window, the cat would probably be startled off the ledge.

Tawny gripped his arm again and Simon tried to reassure her. "Just stay calm."

"I'm going out there after him," she said.

"Bloody hell you are."

"I can't just leave him."

"I'll get him."

"No. I can't let you do that. And he doesn't know you anyway."

Over his dead body was she going out on that wet ledge. He looked down—all seven floors down—and it might very well be his dead body—but no way, no how was he letting her go.

"Panicked animals respond better to strangers in a rescue situation. I saw it on Animal Planet." Total, absolute codswallop—to borrow Grandpa Dickie's favorite expression—and he'd lie again to keep her off the ledge. He edged her out of the window frame and back into the bedroom.

"Wait here and I'll hand him to you." He didn't give her a chance to argue. He climbed out of the window and onto the ledge. It was far narrower than it had appeared from inside.

He gripped the window frame with his left hand

and slowly stood, struggling to maintain his balance. He braced his right hand against the rough brick, wishing the ledge was made of the same instead of slick, wet marble. He hugged the building.

He made the mistake of glancing down. Vertigo rocked him. Head swimming, he teetered and then regained his balance. Fuck. Fuck. Fuck. He didn't like heights worth a damn.

"Simon, get back in here," Tawny said, her head shoved out the window, near his knee.

"I will when I get the cat." He kept his eyes trained on the building and Peaches.

"How are you going to do that?"

She'd picked a jolly time and place for a conversation. "I don't know. I'm working on a plan now."

"Don't you think you should've thought about it before you went out there?"

"I think best under pressure." More codswallop.

He edged toward Peaches, and his towel—the knot loosened by this climb out the window—inched down his hips. Lovely. He was only wearing a towel and it was falling off. Moving very slowly and carefully, he took it off and draped it over one shoulder. Better to hang his bare butt over a ledge than get tripped up by a towel.

Fuck again. He wasn't even going to die with dignity. Honor perhaps but no dignity.

Buck up. Grow a spine. He could do this. The key

to not dying was to move slow and steady. At least, he hoped so.

And he had about a snowball's chance in hell of getting this cat. The bloody beast had swatted at him earlier when he'd tried to pet it. Simon did the only thing he knew to do—he kept sidling toward the cat and talked to it man-to-man…er, man-to-cat, in a low croon.

"Okay, mate. Just hang tight. See, this is the deal. You might have nine lives, but I've only got one…."

"What?" Tawny asked.

He carefully turned his head in her direction. "Just talking to the cat. Give us a minute, okay? And no noise and sudden movement would be most appreciated."

He looked back toward Peaches and pattered on. "Quite frankly I think I'm too young to die, but even if I'm not, pavement diving naked isn't exactly the way I wanted to go. And who knows, you might've used up your lives already."

The cat gave another hair-raising yowl. A whisper of a breeze chilled the sweat trickling between Simon's shoulder blades.

"Listen, I've got a deal for you. Just hear me out. I pick you up, we go back in there and I swear I'll get her to give you another name. Peaches… I might be out here, too, if I had to live with that. But on my honor, you'll be renamed as soon as my bare butt climbs back through that window with you."

Peaches flattened his ears. Te-bloody-rrific. That wasn't a good sign.

Simon was almost there…just a few more inches…

"I'm going to step over you, you know, to get to the other side."

Simon sucked in a deep breath. It was do or die and he didn't like door number two. He raised his right foot and stepped over the cat, which left him straddling Peaches on the ledge, somewhat spread-eagled but at least he could hold on to the window frame and screen of Tawny's next-door neighbor.

He glanced down at the cat. The cat looked up at Simon. Or, more specifically, parts of him. Peaches eyed Simon's willy dangling in the wind with a wicked gleam in his kitty eyes, as if he'd just discovered a newfangled cat toy.

"Don't even think about it." Simon cupped a protective hand over Mr. Winky.

Suddenly an older woman appeared in the window.

"Pervert!" she yelled.

She yanked her window shade down, in his face.

Startled, Simon teetered. He dug his fingers into the window frame. Whoa!

Steady. Steady.

Only in New York.

He recentered and lifted his left foot over the cat. Whew! He unhanded the family jewels. Now for the really scary part—as if he hadn't been scared witless up to this point.

"I'm going to pick you up in this towel. Here's the tricky part. I need for you to be really still or I'm going to lose my balance and we're both going to splat—not a good ending."

He shifted the towel from his shoulder to his hands.

"Easy, there. Just remember, you get a new name. Something cool. Something macho. Something bad-ass to go with your image." While he talked, he leaned down and oh-so-carefully wrapped the cat in the towel. "Stay cool. We're just a minute away from you having a new lease on life and me still *having* a life."

Amazingly Peaches offered no resistence and didn't squirm when he tucked him beneath his arm football-style. Simon had no idea how long it took— it felt like hours—but he continued to talk trash and edge toward Tawny's window. Finally he handed the cat through the window. Tawny snatched The Cat Who'd Earned a New Name and clutched him to her. Simon used his free hand to grip the edge of the open window.

"Do you need help getting in?" Tawny asked.

"Just give me some room." Simon climbed in feetfirst.

With solid flooring beneath him and the windowsill behind him, his knees began to shake. Being confined by four walls had never felt so good! He turned around, slammed the window closed and locked it. They'd roast like swine in hell before he opened that window again.

He turned around just as Peaches…er, Him…lost his patience for being held, leaped out of Tawny's arms and shot into the other room.

He still hadn't recovered his breath when Tawny rounded on him, her eyes flashing, her hair sticking out at odd angles, as if she'd been in a brawl and it'd been nearly pulled out.

"That was the most stupid, idiotic thing I've ever seen," she yelled.

Huh? "What the hell? How about a thank-you?"

"Thank you? Thank you?" Her voice escalated with each *thank you*, which he really hadn't thought was possible. "I should *thank you* when you could've died out there, you idiot?" She flew at him and pummeled him on the chest. "You could've fallen. I was so scared. And you were naked. And you could've died."

God, she was nearly hysterical over *him*. He caught her wrists and tried not to hurt her. "Shh. Shh. It's okay. I'm okay. I'm fine. You're fine. We're fine."

We? Where had that come from?

She leaned her head against his chest. He ran his hand soothingly over her hair. She reached up and wrapped her arms around his neck, pulling him tighter, harder against her, as if she couldn't get close enough. "Never do anything like that again. I've never been so scared in my life. If you'd fallen…"

Her mouth latched on to his and she kissed him with all the passion aroused by fear and anger. She ground her mouth against his, unleashing his own post-window-ledge adrenaline surge. She waged war with her tongue. He kissed her back as if he was devouring her.

Dammit. He *could've* died out there. He hadn't been sure that he wouldn't until he'd slammed the window closed behind him. But he hadn't died and she was in his arms. And she cared, tremendously it would seem, that he'd risked his life.

They stumbled the few feet to the bed, both of them trying to eat the other alive. They fell to the mattress. This time Simon fished in the drawer for a condom, his hand shaking. He'd wanted her before, burned for her, dreamed of her, made love to her, but he'd never known anything like this—the overwhelming consuming need to bury himself so far and hard within her, to celebrate having come in off that ledge, to claim her.

While he put on the condom, she pulled off her panties and top and fell back, legs spread, sex glistening, ready.

"No. Roll over. On your knees."

She stayed on her back but closed her legs, a mutinous expression on her face. Wrong direction.

"No. Not until you blow out all the candles," she said.

She wasn't exactly the most logical woman he'd ever met. "But you're afraid of the dark."

"I'm even more afraid of how big my butt is. And time's wasting." She reached out and wrapped her fingers around him and stroked.

Damn, it felt good, but he was made of sterner stuff than that.

He pulled away from her and dropped to his knees beside the bed. She eyed him with suspicion and a fair measure of frustration.

"I'm here to worship at the altar of your magnificent to-die-for bum. Why do you really think I crawled out on that ledge? For the cat? So that I could gaze into your green eyes afterward? So you could try to beat the bloody hell out of me when I completed my mission? Oh, no, luv. I climbed out there for this." He stroked the curve of her magnificent bottom and sank his hands into her cheeks. She looked torn between laughing and smacking him, but luckily she still had that I-want-to-screw-your-brains-out glint in her eyes.

"I said it earlier, this—" he stroked the curve of her rear "—could bring men to their knees. See. I'm on my knees. And I'd like you on your knees, in as much light as possible so I can enjoy not just the feel and the taste but the sight of this fine masterpiece in action."

He wasn't giving up on this. Not only was every word true—he wanted to see her jiggle and wiggle while he pumped into her from behind—but he also wanted her to get over this self-consciousness, wanted her to realize her behind was a cause for celebration, not something to hide in the dark and make derogatory comments about.

He nuzzled the soft flesh in question. Fully convinced actions spoke louder than words, he devoted himself to showing her how much he appreciated her assets. He took his time kissing…licking…sucking his way across her sweet terrain. She rewarded him with low moans of appreciation, squirming against his mouth.

He was on fire for her—he did have a major attachment to her rear and the musky scent of her arousal was maddening, the moisture seeping between her nether lips…. He culled a taste of her sweet nectar with his tongue.

"Simon…"

He looked at her flushed face from his vantage point between her thighs.

"Would you really deny me something that would make me so happy?"

Panting, frantic, hot, she rolled over so quickly it took him by surprise. He got to his feet and she was already on her knees, legs spread, her rounded cheeks thrust in the air, her bare sex glistening a wet invitation.

"You're driving me crazy. We'll do it your way. But just do it." She looked at him over her shoulder and slapped one full, luscious cheek. "If this is what you want, mount up and ride 'em, cowboy!"

Bloody right—he was a cowboy on a pilgrimage. Simon climbed on the bed behind her. He skimmed one finger between her cheeks. "I've approached the temple of the divine. May I enter?"

"Dammit, Simon. It's just not right for you to make me laugh when you've made me so horny."

He slid his condom-covered erection along her slick channel and rubbed it against her clit. "I'd like to offer up my sacrifice."

She thrust back against him and he finished the job, plunging into her, his hands grasping her hips.

"Yessss," she cried. "I'm happy. Are you happy now?"

She was hot and tight, and he settled into the rhythm of their ride and spoke while he was still capable of speech.

"No. I'm ecstatic."

"YOU WANT ME TO DO WHAT? Forget it. I'm not doing it," Tawny said and rolled to her back, huffing out her breath. Damnation, here she was feeling boneless and fabulous after really, really hot sex and now Simon had to go ruin it.

Simon rolled off the side of the bed, graceful, all leashed power and controlled muscles, and headed for the door. Annoyed with him or not, she'd be content to watch him walk around naked for a really long time— except he was walking out the door.

"Where are you going?" she asked.

"To get my camera."

"You need your camera to discuss this?"

"No. I need my camera to catch what you look like in a pout. Remember, I'm supposed to be capturing the real you."

"That was a jerk thing to say," she yelled after him.

"Sorry." Sorry, her well-ridden ass. He didn't sound sorry a bit. "It's my specialty," he called from the other room.

"What? Photography or being a jerk?" she muttered to herself, thoroughly put out with him.

"I heard that." He reappeared in the door, wearing his jeans but shirtless, camera around his neck. "Both."

"I'll second that."

He approached the bed, the camera whirring. She tossed him a disgusted, haughty look, stuck her nose in the air and looked the other way.

"Perfect. Tawny in a sulk."

She whipped her head back around. "I am *not* in a sulk."

"Really? What would you call it?"

"Pissed. I'm pissed. You had no right to promise my cat I'd change his name. I love his name. You want to name a pet, go get one yourself," she said.

She could give a rat's patootie if she sounded rude. All her life she'd been told what to do, when to do it, how to do it. Finally she was on her own and she'd be damned if *anyone*—regardless how good he looked naked or how thoroughly he satisfied her in bed—was arbitrarily renaming her cat. Peaches was the first thing she'd ever had on her own that was all hers. Simon could stuff it.

"I was desperate. It was the only thing I could think of out there. And I gave him my word."

"Well, you should've checked with me first."

"What? I should've conducted negotiations from the window ledge, where I just happened to be hanging out naked?"

"There's no need for sarcasm, Simon."

"There's no need for irrationality, Tawny."

She *would* let that comment pass, 'cause the other option was to kill him. And to think she'd actually begun to like him. Ugh. He infuriated her.

"Did I ask you to go out there? No! In fact, I told you not to."

"You really thought I'd let *you* go out there?"

Tawny couldn't recall ever sputtering before in her life, ever being so spitting mad she couldn't verbally express herself. Not even that lifetime ago when she'd found out Elliott had swung to the other side.

"Uh…uh…you…you…absolute macho…do you think just because you're a man that you're braver?"

"Brave?" He threw back his head and laughed, but it didn't sound as if he was particularly amused. "Bravery had nothing to do with it. I was so bloody scared I couldn't see straight out there. And you can hang up the macho thing because Mr. Macho wouldn't admit that."

"And *I'm* irrational? Hah! If you were scared, why didn't you just let me go?"

"Because I couldn't…it just seemed like the thing to do."

He walked out of the bedroom. Typical male to just walk away in the middle of a conversation that wasn't going his way.

Tawny yanked on her panties and tank top and marched down the hall after him.

"Well, there's an explanation. That really clears it up for me. Thank you," she said.

"Can't you ever just drop anything?" Simon sat on the couch.

If he thought he could get rid of her or shut her up by holing up in this claustrophobic little den...well, he was wrong. She plopped down on the other end of the sofa.

"No, Simon, I can't. So shoot me if I like a little logic in my life."

"Righto! You're not exactly the most logical woman I ever met."

He *must* be kidding! "That's rich—especially coming from a man who climbed out naked on a window ledge and promised to change my cat's name—without my permission, I might add—because it seemed like the thing to do. Oh, yeah. You're the king of logic."

"You want logic? Try this on. I went out there because if I didn't, you would, and I couldn't bear it if something happened to you." He snapped his mouth shut, as if he'd said too much. And well, really, he'd just said a lot.

Simon had gone out there because he was worried

about *her?* Warmth that had nothing to do with sex and everything to do with emotion suffused her. It hadn't been all about him—making him look brave and macho. His climbing out on the ledge had been about *her.*

"Oh," she said rather dumbly.

"So I'm sorry that you're annoyed, but I promised him a new name."

Simon wasn't just a control freak intent on running her business. Guilt displaced her anger. "Maybe I did overreact just a little to all of that."

"Maybe you did. How would you like to be this big, bad-attitude cat with a name like Peaches?" He shuddered.

Really, he didn't have to sound so disdainful and he could drop the theatrics. "It's not as if I single-handedly emasculated him."

Simon reached along the back of the sofa and trailed his fingers along her shoulder. "No. The vet helped, but that name does a fine job."

"Okay. Let's hear you do better. Whatcha got?"

"Sorry?" His blank look struck her as rather comical and cute. She didn't think Simon often looked blank.

"Names," she prompted. "It was your idea. *You* come up with a name for him."

"It's your cat."

"According to some ancient cultures, since you saved his life, he essentially belongs to you now."

"But I don't want him." He looked horrified at the prospect.

"I'm not literally giving him to you. Think figuratively. I'm giving you the task of naming him."

"But I don't want to."

"Tough. You promised him a new name…so give him one."

"But I don't know anything about naming animals."

She rolled her eyes. God. He was sexy and insane and exasperating. "What do you mean you don't know how to name an animal? You just do it. Haven't you ever had a pet?"

He crossed his arms over his chest. "No."

He was pulling her leg. "No cats, dogs, gerbils, guinea pigs when you were growing up?"

"No."

She moved down the pet chain to a group she didn't exactly consider petworthy. You just couldn't cuddle a reptile. "Not even a lizard or snake or…maybe a frog?"

"No pets."

A lightbulb lit up in her head. "Let me guess… your parents."

"They weren't into pets."

Tawny ground her teeth, endangering thousands of dollars of orthodontia her parents had sunk into her pearly whites. What kind of people emotionally neglected their kid and to top it off denied him a pet? Even the very proper Edwards household had included a dog, a hamster and several goldfish over the years. A frog would've been better than nothing. "Let me guess again. A pet would be too much trouble?"

"Righto."

"I really dislike your parents." She ached to give them a piece of her mind.

Simon looked startled, as if surprised she'd take exception with his parents on his behalf. Then he grinned. *Wow!* He should grin more often.

"Don't worry," he said, "they wouldn't be charmed by you either. You're too…unleashed for them."

"Unleashed? I like that." And she'd be frightened if those people *did* like her. "Don't think you're weaseling out of renaming Peaches. You either name him or he will forever be Peaches and you'll have reneged on your promise."

"You're a hard woman, Tawny Edwards."

"Humph. I'm just forcing you to put your…whatever…where your mouth is."

"Brutus." He smirked.

"Uh-uh. I can't live with a cat named Brutus. Try again."

"Magnus." An even bigger smirk.

Okay. She'd play his game…and beat him at it. "Forget it. I just had a stroke of genius. And it is a stroke of genius if you consider how ornery and standoffish and generally difficult he is. Instead of you naming him, I'll name him for you."

"Fine with me. What's his new name?" The smirk gave way to trepidation. He should be leery.

"Simon. I'm naming him after you."

"Didn't you just mention ornery and contrary and generally difficult?"

"Exactly. If the shoe fits…"

Oddly enough, Simon didn't appear leery or confounded or in the least put out. Who'd have thought it? The crazy man looked extremely pleased at having a cat named after him.

"HE SEEMS HAPPY WITH THE new name. What do you think?" Tawny said.

Simon the cat, formerly known as Peaches, sat atop the refrigerator, eyes closed, patently ignoring them. Simon the man thought Tawny was crazy, totally irrational and altogether adorable. "I'd say he's beside himself."

Tawny shook her head and sent him a chastising look. "I know him better than you do and I say he's happy."

"Whatever you say. I promised him a macho name and I'm fairly certain Simon doesn't fall into that category," he argued, knowing it was futile.

Tawny laughed and Simon mentally took a snapshot. He wanted to remember this moment forever. They were engaged in a totally inane conversation in her oven of a kitchen with no electricity and he couldn't recall ever feeling happier than he did at this moment.

"Like Magnus was boss? Yeah."

"You know, you could give a guy a complex," he said.

"Better watch out or you might turn out gay like Elliott," she said, obviously joking but obviously still smarting from Elliott's revelation.

"Not a remote possibility. I know you're having me on, but Elliott's sexual preference is no reflection on you." He smiled and allowed himself to look at her with the familiarity of a well-satisfied lover. "I know firsthand."

She stood on tiptoe and brushed her lips against his cheek, her hand resting lightly on his shoulder. "Thanks. Whether you like to admit it or not, you're really a very nice man."

Her tenderness shook him. "Didn't you call me a jerk not too long ago?"

"They're not mutually exclusive. You can be that, too."

The way she looked at him—as if he'd hung the moon—left his mouth dry and his heart pounding. She was wrong. She might think she knew him, but she didn't. He was ninety-nine percent jerk ninety-nine percent of the time. She was rebounding big-time and painting him to be someone he wasn't.

"You're going to have to talk to Elliott, Tawny."

"Technically I don't have to do anything…but, I suppose I will."

"You'll need closure on it or you'll be tracking him down because you'll have that Prozac addiction," he said. She was too easy to be with. Too easy to tease.

"You know me too well." She threw a dish towel at his head.

He caught it one-handed. "You seem to be handling it well."

"I'm not prone to hysterics."

He quirked an eyebrow, recalling the scene she'd made when he'd come back through the window earlier. She'd verged on hysteria. Over him. He was still reeling.

"Okay. Well, thinking you're about to see someone you care—know—die, that's a little different. But as a rule I don't get hysterical." She looked him over from head to toe, her gaze lingering at the front of his trousers. "And you've definitely helped ease my rejection pain."

"Glad to be of service." And he'd be up for more service if she didn't stop eyeing his crotch that way.

"You may think, *yeah, right,* but I'm almost relieved. Not that Elliott's gay and not that he decided to screw around on me—that's a little tough to take—but I think both of us knew something wasn't working. And then when I started having those dreams about you…well, it does sort of make a girl think she's not quite ready to tie the knot."

He was still floored he'd been the object of this woman's fantasy—even if she had been unconscious at the time.

"Dreams are a pretty iffy indicator," he said. "Would you have called it off if Elliott hadn't gotten involved with someone else?"

She considered his question for a few seconds, her lips pursed, before she pushed her hair back from her face. "I don't know. Probably. Hopefully. I don't hate him, although I came pretty close when you told me. I'm less than impressed with his cheating and then dumping it on you to tell me."

"Do you still love him? You obviously did at one point." The question tied his belly in knots.

"I'm not sure." She nudged the spot on her finger where her ring had been with her thumb. He was sure she didn't realize what she was doing. "I did love him. Actually I think when I'm over being so pissed, I still do." His stomach plummeted. "But I don't love him the way I should to marry him. We have fun together, but there's no real passion between us—" her gaze snared him, trapped him with the banked fires within their depth "—no intensity. Do you know what I mean?"

He looked away before she saw the answering fire in his eyes. "The mention of his name ties you up in knots? You'd go to hell and back again if you thought he needed you? The sound of his voice sends shivers through you? I know exactly what you mean."

"Elliott and I don't have that."

Granted, she was a grown woman and could make her own decisions. But at one point she'd been sure enough to agree to marry Elliott. He knew first-hand she could be wildly emotional and illogical and he didn't want to see her make a decision she'd later regret.

"Passion doesn't last. It burns out and evolves in-to something else altogether," he said, playing dev-il's advocate.

"I'm not naive. I don't think people still have that after twenty years. Or—who knows?—maybe they do. But you should definitely have it in the beginning. Love shouldn't be totally comfortable, like an old pair of slippers. It should be like a pair of stilettos— sexy and exciting and worth the discomfort. And if that's what Elliott's found, more power to him." She shrugged and smiled.

Her smile was so her—natural, irrepressible, sun-ny—he couldn't help smiling in return.

"That's an original. I've never heard love com-pared to a pair of stilettos."

"I didn't realize I felt this way until…well, I think it started with those dreams, and now this with Elliott has forced me to reevaluate everything. And I can't help it if you think I'm being tacky when I say the sex between us, you and me, has been pretty incredible."

He'd have to be dead or stupid not to feel a surge of male pride that he'd rocked her world to a degree that Elliott obviously hadn't. He was fairly sure he wore the village idiot's grin. "It has been, hasn't it?"

"While we're discussing Elliott…I want you to

know I have no intention of mentioning what happened tonight to him…you know…us."

That wiped the grin off his face. "Because you're ashamed?"

"No." She shot him a look that said he knew better. "Because he's your friend and I don't want to come between you. But even more than that, because I don't want you to think I slept with you to get back at him. I slept with you because you drove me crazy in my dreams and then when you got here…it was even worse."

"Worse?"

"You know what I mean. The sound of your voice, the touch of your hands on my shoulders, your scent." All the hallmarks of passion.

She aroused him without even touching him. And there was only one logical response to that.

Simon backed her up against the counter and kissed her.

9

TAWNY RAN HER HANDS OVER Simon's sweat-slicked chest. Making out had definitely raised her temperature, but it was like a furnace in the kitchen.

Something she'd read in a magazine once and filed for future reference came to mind. Now seemed like the perfect time to try it.

"How about a Popsicle? If the electricity's off much longer they're going to melt anyway. At least it'll be cool."

He moved so that she was no longer wedged between the counter and his hard—and some parts getting harder—body. "Sure. I haven't had a Popsicle in years."

"I keep them stocked when it's this hot. Sort of a sweet fix without all the calories." She opened the freezer and pulled out a box. "Great. They're still frozen. Cherry, strawberry or grape?"

"Definitely cherry."

She passed one to him. "That's my favorite, too."

She returned the box to the freezer.

She'd told him it would cool him down—but not

before she heated him up. She peeled off the wrapper. Slowly, making a sensual production of it, she licked up one side and down the other. "Mmm." Looking up at him, she deliberately took the Popsicle into her mouth and sucked, moving her head up and down over the frozen treat. She moaned in the back of her throat.

Simon stood transfixed, clutching his Popsicle in his hand. "I'm not sure I can watch you eat that without having a heart attack." He leaned against the counter, as if he was equally unsure his legs would support him.

Tawny smiled and nibbled at the tip. She was really getting off on how much she was turning him on. Turning both of them on. She slid her tank top down over her shoulders and pulled the front down, freeing her breasts. "Well, then, how does this work for you?" She trailed the Popsicle over her nipples. The icy cold felt incredible against her skin, the sensation shooting through her. "Wow! Guaranteed to cool you down quick."

Simon made a choked noise. "Tawny…"

There was a definite bulge straining the front of his jeans.

"Want to take our treat to the bedroom? I think it might be more comfortable in there." And she had no intention of having Popsicle sex—or any other sex, for that matter—in front of her cat. She snagged a bowl.

"Let's go." He grabbed her hand and damn near dragged her down the hall and into the bedroom.

"Mmm. I like a man with enthusiasm."

"You and your Popsicle have definitely aroused my *enthusiasm*," he said.

Laughing, she scooped up the towel he'd worn out onto the ledge from the floor, spread it on the bed and sat down on the edge.

Simon reached for her and she backed him off. "Enthusiasm's one thing, but impatience is another. It's not time yet. We've only begun to enjoy our Popsicles."

She trailed it back over her nipples—God, it did feel incredible—and then over her belly and across the tops of her thighs.

"Luv, please…"

She felt like such a wicked woman. And she loved it. She was dripping wet and it wasn't sweat. "I can tell you where I really need cooling down…."

She lay back, leaning on one elbow, and spread her legs. She propped one foot up on the mattress, leaving herself open, giving Simon a visual of just how wet she was already.

"Tawny…" Simon said, part groan and all appreciation. His low, faintly accented voice slid over her, arousing her even more.

The kiss of the ice against her inner thigh zinged through her. Slowly she rimmed the frozen treat along her vagina, the sensation deliciously arousing.

She felt thoroughly wicked and thoroughly excited. She eased the melting Popsicle in and twirled it around.

"Ooh." It was hard and icy and she was so hot. Simon never looked away from her as he unzipped and took off his pants. She worked the melting ice in and out and licked her lips.

Simon walked over to the edge of the bed. "Suck on mine." She was so close, she could've come with very little effort when he used that erotic, commanding tone. He teased it along her lips and then slid it into her mouth. She moved the icy-cold Popsicle in and out of her vagina and he matched the rhythm in her mouth.

Tawny wasn't sure that she'd ever been so turned on in her life. She was so hot inside, she was melting the Popsicle in record time, deliciously cold against her inferno. And the look on Simon's face...

She slid her mouth off his Popsicle and licked leisurely down the length of it. "You look hot—" she eyed his straining erection "—and uncomfortable. I've got just the thing to cool you down. Cold on the surface, hot inside."

Simon didn't need a second invite. He rolled on a condom and in one smooth stroke he was in.

"Oh my God." Tawny wasn't sure which one of them said it. Maybe both. Maybe neither. Had anything ever felt as good as his hot cock against her icy-cold flesh? Hot and cold. Hard and soft.

It felt too good...she was so hot...she wasn't going to last any longer.

Popsicle sex with Simon—guaranteed to come in three minutes or less.

SIMON STARTLED AWAKE. It took him a second to figure out his cell phone was ringing in his pants somewhere on the dark floor. He slung his legs over the side of the bed and reached down, groping for his jeans.

By the time he found them, he'd missed he call. He glanced at his watch. Who the hell was calling him at this hour in the morning?

Tawny leaned up on one arm. "Hmm. Who's on the phone?"

"I'm checking now." He listened to his voice mail. "Simon, it's your father. Call me back at…wait, you can't call me here." He'd hung up. What the— His parents never called him.

"It was my dad," Simon said to Tawny, who had sat up, wide-awake now. "First he asked me to call him back and then he said I couldn't call him where he was. But I'm going to try anyway." Apprehension flooded him. Whatever this was, it couldn't be good.

Before he could hit Send to call the number shown on the display, his phone rang again. Same number flashed across the screen.

Simon answered. "Dad?"

"Simon, thank God you answered. I'm at City North Hospital. We think your mother's had a heart attack."

His father's words struck him like a physical blow. He sank to the edge of the bed. "Where is she now?"

"Here at City North."

"No." Simon bit back his impatience. "Is she in ICU?"

"No. They're running an EKG in the emergency room and checking her enzymes. She needs for you to come, Simon." There was a pregnant pause. "I need for you to come."

Simon didn't hesitate. For better or worse, they were his parents. They were all each of them had. "I'll be there. It may take me a while, but I'm on my way. I'll have my cell with me. Call me if anything changes."

He hung up. In a detached, remote way, as if observing another person, he noticed his hands were shaking.

"What is it? What's the matter?"

"My mother's had a heart attack." Speaking the words aloud left him nauseous. He dropped to the edge of the bed, uncertain his legs would support him.

"Oh, Simon." Tawny hugged him from behind, her arms offering comfort from one human being to another. "Which hospital?"

"City North."

She released him and got out of the bed. She yanked open a dresser drawer and stepped into a pair of running shorts. Simon pulled on his jeans and T-shirt. Without any self-consciousness she pulled off her tank top and donned a heavy-duty exercise bra.

"What are you doing?" he asked.

"What does it look like I'm doing? I'm getting

dressed. City North is northwest of here. I don't have a car and I don't know if we can find a cab at this time in the morning, but we could run it—" she glanced to where he sat on the edge of the bed lacing his Doc Martens "—if you think you can in those boots. Unfortunately none of my shoes would fit you."

"We?"

A few quick brushstrokes and she pulled her hair up into a ponytail. She looked at him in the dresser mirror. "I'm coming with you."

"That's not necessary." He stood and tucked in his shirt, zipped his pants.

"Yes, it is." She pulled on a running singlet.

"What if I don't want you to come?"

"Are you telling me you don't want me there?"

The trouble was, it frightened him just how much he *did* want her there. Scary how easy it was to want to lean on her when he'd stood alone so long on his own. And what did it matter whether he actually wanted her there or not? He knew Tawny. She'd be there regardless.

"Oh, hell. Come if you want to," he said.

"You're so gracious, Simon." She pressed a quick kiss to his cheek. "But I forgive you. I know you're worried about your mom."

She buzzed around the room, pulling a small canister out of her seemingly bottomless bedside table and clipping it to her waistband. "Mace. A girl should never leave home without it." She shoved her feet into trainers and laced them up in quick order.

She stopped and looked at him. "You ready?"

"Yeah. You're sure you know where we're going?" He wanted to be there now.

"Positive. I've got a great sense of direction."

"That's good. I have no sense of direction." Simon lit a small votive and blew out the triple-wicked big boy. Votive in hand, he led the way to the front door. Tawny blew out the two candles she'd previously left burning in the den. Her apartment felt like an oven. They hadn't even started their run and sweat beaded his skin.

She joined him at the door, clipping on her cell phone. "Just blow it out and leave it here. It'll slow us down too much in the stairwell."

He grabbed her and pressed a quick kiss to her surprised mouth. She was scared to death of the dark, but she didn't want to slow him down in getting to his mother.

"You're one hell of a woman, Tawny Edwards. Let's keep it lit for the first set of stairs, so we can count how many are from landing to landing. Then if it goes out, we can count our way down in the dark."

"Sounds like a plan." They stepped out into the hallway and she dead-bolted the door behind them. "The stairwell's this way."

She grabbed his free hand and led him down the dark hall. Simon opened the heavy door beneath the dark Exit sign. The door slammed shut behind them, leaving them in the dank cool and eery quiet of the stairwell.

Simon gripped Tawny's hand even tighter. God, she must hate this. And it was about to get worse.

"Ready?" His voice bounced back at them.

"Let's do it."

He counted aloud as they went down one floor. Only six floors left to go. The candle had flickered precariously several times on the way down the last set of stairs and they hadn't even been moving that fast. It would take them forever at this rate.

Tawny stopped him on the sixth-floor landing. "Just blow it out, Simon."

"Are you sure?"

She took a deep breath. "You'll hold on to my hand?"

"I promise I won't let go of you, no matter what happens."

"Then let's move out." She leaned around him and blew out the votive, pitching them into absolute blackness. According to fire code, emergency exit lights should've shown up over the doorways. Obviously Tawny's building had compliance issues.

They made their way tentatively at first and then fell into a rhythm. Simon counted aloud, his voice echoing, but he thought it was some measure of comfort to Tawny to hear his voice and hold his hand in the inky black. Soon enough they'd reached the first floor.

It hadn't taken long at all, but it had probably felt like a lifetime to Tawny, judging by her clammy hand.

Muggy heat assaulted them the moment they stepped out of the building. A few quiet voices drifted down from rooftops and fire escapes, and somewhere down the block a woman laughed. In the far distance a horn honked. The earlier party atmosphere had definitely dissipated.

"It's like a fairy tale where a spell's been cast, isn't it?" she asked, dropping into a lunge to stretch.

Simon moved through his own prerun stretches. He knew exactly what she meant. The city that never slept lay about them in uneasy slumber.

"It's like the proverbial sleeping giant, isn't it?" he said.

"Exactly. Listen, I know you're anxious to get there, but remember it's six miles. Let's pace it. I believe she's going to be fine, Simon. At least she's at the hospital and in good hands."

"You lead and I'll be right there with you."

Tawny headed east through the darkness toward New Jersey and Simon followed. At the corner, where a flower shop stood in silent bloom, she turned north. Simon reminded himself to match her stride. They ran in companionable silence for several blocks, only passing a few cars and the occasional pedestrian.

He needed this, to run, to push himself. Inside he was a mess. So he wasn't close to his parents. In many ways their relationship bordered on hostile. But he didn't want anything to happen to his mother. She wasn't exactly a nurturer, but he hadn't exactly tried to reach out to them either. At least, not in a long time. He'd summarily ignored their occasional overtures in the last couple of years.

Running through the dark, silent streets, he gave voice to the emotions racking his soul. Tawny would understand.

"I shouldn't feel this resentment. This situation should absolve it. I should let it go, Tawny, but I can't. Dammit, I can't let it go. It's always been the two of them, with me on the outside looking in. They had each other and I had my resentment. It was my companion during my childhood and while I was a teenager. All these years I've nurtured it, embraced it, and I can't abandon it now. But the really crazy part is, I love her so desperately…." He trailed off, conflicted, close to weeping.

"Of course you do. She's your mother. And you can resent the hell out of both of them, but it doesn't mean you don't love them. It's our job to be screwed up by our parents. They screwed us up. We'll screw our kids up. It's one of those unwritten laws of nature. But it doesn't mean they don't love you and it doesn't mean you don't love them."

Her words soothed his troubled soul as the night's oppressive heat absorbed the rhythmic pounding of their feet. Simon ignored the biting sting of a blister on his left heel. Doc Martens weren't optimal running footwear. Amazing how just talking to her made him feel better.

"How'd you get to be so smart?" he asked.

Her answer was lost when a spotlight fixed on them and a voice rang out.

"Stop. Police."

Tawny stumbled and Simon caught her arm, steadying her. They stopped and stood on the sidewalk, sides heaving, waiting.

Blinded by the light, they only heard the slam of a car door and approaching footsteps. "What seems to be the hurry? Kind of odd to be running in the middle of the night dressed all in black? You running from something or someone in particular?"

Piss if he needed some cop with a bad attitude. Didn't this guy have anything better to do? "Don't you have anything—"

Tawny stepped on his foot and cut him off. "Morning, Officer." Her Southern drawl rolled out, thick and sweet as molasses. "We're on our way to City North Hospital. Simon's mother's had a heart attack. I don't have a car and no cabs are out, so we've run all the way." Tawny smiled at the officer, who remained a faceless silhouette against the blinding light. "I know it looks odd, but Simon didn't have any running clothes at my apartment, which is why he's running in all black."

"Where are you from?"

Jesus, it was an ungodly hour, hotter than hell, they were in the middle of a blackout and this guy— this *cop*—was flirting with her. Give him a break.

"Savannah, originally."

"Ah, a Georgia peach."

Tawny laughed, that warm, husky laugh that crawled over his skin and turned him inside out. "And you sound like a New York boy."

"Born and raised. Hey, whaddaya say I give the two of you a ride to the hospital?"

Earlier she'd accused Simon of being macho, and really he never had been. But now he had the over-whelming urge to tell this guy to take his ride and shove it up...

"That'd be lovely. We'd really appreciate getting to the hospital as quickly as possible. Wouldn't we, Simon?" She stepped on his foot again.

"Uh, yeah. The sooner the better."

"I'm afraid you'll both have to sit in the back." The cop gave Tawny a look of apology. "Regula-tions. Only a badge can sit up front."

"The back is fine." She stepped over the uneven sidewalk and tugged Simon toward the car. New York's own Dudley Do-Right opened the rear door. Tawny offered him a smile that probably curled his insides. It would've curled Simon's if it'd been di-rected at him. "This is so nice of you," she said, climbing in the back, her running shorts hugging ev-ery delicious curve of her sweet bottom. And yeah, the dickhead wearing the badge noticed. Simon crawled into the back seat behind her. A steel cage separated them from the front. He'd never been in a police cruiser before. The radio squawked and the officer relayed his twenty—his location—and where he was heading.

Tawny held fast to Simon's hand while she carried on a conversation with Dan Berthold, their officer-chauffeur. With the streets virtually deserted, Officer Berthold didn't seem to mind breaking the law he was sworn to uphold, and within minutes they pulled up to the hospital that stood like a beacon of light in a surrounding sea of dark.

"Would you mind dropping us at the E.R.?" Tawny asked.

"No problem," Berthold swung around to the emergency-room entrance, threw the car in park and jumped out to open the back door.

Simon didn't miss the way the cop eyed Tawny's legs as she climbed out. Simon quelled the urge to knock him flat. Assaulting an officer who'd just delivered him to his mother seemed a bad idea—even if he deserved it for looking at Tawny like that.

Tawny shook Berthold's hand. "Thank you so much. I know why you're called New York's finest."

"You want me to wait? I could wait."

"That's really sweet, but we don't know how long we'll be. Thanks so much."

"My pleasure." Berthold turned to Simon. "Hope she's okay, man." He held out a hand.

Simon took his proffered hand and shook it. Maybe the guy wasn't so bad after all. He hadn't really hit on Tawny and they had arrived a hell of a lot faster than running. "Thanks for the ride."

"Anytime." With a final appreciative glance at Tawny's derriere in her running shorts, Berthold got in his car and left.

"He had the hots for you."

Tawny rolled her eyes at him. "He got us here fifteen minutes earlier than if we'd run the whole way." She started toward the double doors. "Come on. When we get inside, don't worry about me. I'll wait in the lobby."

Simon stopped on the sidewalk outside the wide emergency-room doors. "No. I want you to come with me."

"I don't mind waiting in the lobby. I don't want to intrude."

He skimmed the line of her jaw with the back of his hand, needing to touch her, admitting what didn't come easily to him. "I'd really like for you to come with me."

She turned her cheek into his touch. "Then I'll go with you." She took his hand in hers. "Let's go find your mother."

They stepped into utter, overwhelming chaos, bright fluorescent lights—all the brighter after the dark—

and the cool bliss of air-conditioning. Simon glanced around, at a loss as to where to go. Tawny dragged him behind her. "What's your mother's name?"

"Letitia. Letitia Marbury. She didn't take my dad's name when they married. Dr. Letitia Marbury."

Tawny marched up to a desk. Within minutes her smile and Southern charm had elicited his mother's location.

Tawny put her hand on his arm. "You go on up. I'd like to freshen up."

"I'll wait." Now that he was here he didn't want to go up, fear at exactly what he'd find stalling him.

"No. Go on up. You need a few minutes alone with them. I'll meet you there in ten minutes." She pressed a kiss to his cheek and pushed him in the general direction of the elevator bank. His sweat-soaked T-shirt chilled beneath the blast of air-conditioning. "I promise I'll be right up." She touched his arm. "Go on, Simon, she's waiting for you."

10

ONCE SIMON DISAPPEARED through the swinging double doors, Tawny headed for the exit. She followed two EMTs wheeling an empty gurney out the door. Ugh. The heat was even worse, coming out of the air-conditioning. She went from cool to sticky and sweaty in about two seconds flat.

She tried to ignore the strands of hair that had escaped her ponytail and lay plastered against her neck, and hauled out her cell phone. Cell-phone usage in an emergency room was one big no-no. She blew out her breath. She wanted to make this call about as much as she wanted another hole in her head. Double not.

She hit the speed-dial number.

He answered on the second ring. "Tawny?"

She jumped in without preamble. "We're at City North Hospital. Simon's mother's had a heart attack. You need to get here as quick as you can." She paced the sidewalk, past a couple sharing a bench and a cigarette.

"But I'm locked in at the gallery," Elliott protested.

"Then get unlocked. Didn't you hear what I just said? Simon's mother's had a heart attack. He needs you. Herc. Now."

"I don't know if—"

Elliott exhausted her patience. "*I know.* I know your very best friend in the world needs you now more than he ever has, and if you have to blow the damned door off the hinges, you better haul your butt down here pronto." An ambulance, lights flashing but siren silent, pulled up to the double doors. "Don't make me come get you, Elliott."

"Tawny—"

"Elliott, I'm not playing with you. If I have to, I *will* come and drag you out of there."

"Hold on a sec."

The back door of the ambulance opened and they wheeled out one very pregnant Hispanic woman. Very pregnant. Very distressed. Now there was something to be thankful for—that she wasn't *that* woman.

Muffled conversation came through the line and then Elliott was back on the phone.

"Richard's coming with me," Elliott said, defiance ringing in his voice.

Whatever. "I don't care if you drag in the whole rainbow coalition, just get here."

"But there aren't any cabs out and the subway's dead."

"Elliott, you're a New Yorker, for God's sake. Walk."

"Be reasonable, Tawny. I'm wearing my Bruno Ms."

If one more man told her to be reasonable to-night… Tawny barely held on to her temper. She wasn't at her most patient when running, literally, on maybe an hour of sleep. "Elliott, I know how fond you are of those shoes and I will personally pay to have them resoled. Now listen to me and listen good. Pretend you aren't the center of the universe. Pretend you care as much about your friend as you do those damn shoes. You put Simon in a helluva position to-night and he covered for you. I don't care if you have to crawl, get here. You've got one hour to show up. I swear to you, if you don't, I will make your life a living hell."

"All right. I'm on my way."

His petulance didn't further endear him.

"And Elliott…"

"Yes?"

"Don't bitch about the shoes when you get here."

She hung up, fairly certain Elliott would drag in within the hour. Nagging him to come through for his friend hadn't been nearly as effective as promising him a life of misery if he was a no-show. And Elliott knew she would.

Tawny turned off her cell and made her way back through the sea of humanity lining the emergency room.

She ducked into a bathroom. Ugh. She hated public toilets. She wrinkled her nose at the antiseptic smell. Must be a prerequisite for hospitals that they use the cleanser with the nauseating stench. Why'd the urge to pee always strike at the most inopportune times?

She did her business and then stood in front of the sink washing her hands. Ew. She was positively frightening. No makeup. Sweaty. Scraggly, greasy hair. Dark circles from lack of sleep. She'd undoubtedly scare small children. She splashed cold water on her face and repaired her hair as best she could, but she still wasn't winning any beauty pageants tonight.

She left the bathroom behind and navigated the labyrinthine halls to the elevator bank. City North was clean and boasted a reputation for excellent care, but it was one of the older hospitals in the city and its elevators ran slowly. Eventually she reached the fourth floor, a relatively quiet hall that wasn't part of Intensive Care—a very good sign for Simon's mom that she was well enough to warrant a regular room. Two nurses sat engrossed in conversation behind the nurses'-station desk. Tawny followed the sign directing her left to the room number they'd been given downstairs.

Her rubber soles squelched on the spotless tile as she walked down the hall.

A distinguished-looking man who bore a striking resemblance to Simon stood outside the door. A little taller than Simon, gray hair, clipped goatee, chinos, a short-sleeved button-down and thick fisherman sandals. Distinguished didn't impress her. Her father and his colleagues were all distinguished and it didn't make them any more or less decent human beings than anyone else.

Tawny drew a deep breath. She needed to ditch the attitude. It wouldn't do anyone any good. This wasn't about her. She was here to support Simon, not mix it up with his parents. So this man hadn't exactly been the father of the year for Simon, but he was still his father. And Simon, despite their history and their obvious shortcomings as parents—definitely just her opinion—cared for them.

They were his parents, regardless of the fact that Simon deserved better ones. Of course, Simon could really use a better friend than Elliott, who'd needed intimidation to bring him here. Simon was sweet and tender and one of the finest men she'd ever met, and he deserved the very best life had to offer.

The man looked up as she approached, eyeing her blankly.

"Mr. Thackeray?" He nodded. "I'm Tawny Edwards, a friend of Simon's." She extended her hand and after a moment's hesitation he shook it.

"Very good. Very good. Charles Thackeray."

"How is Dr. Marbury?"

He passed a weary hand over his face. "Stable. She's resting comfortably now that Simon's here."

His obvious weariness dispelled some of her harbored animosity. Good parent or bad parent, here was a man worried about the woman he loved.

"He ran almost six miles to get here." She thought he should know.

He looked taken aback. "He ran?"

"Yes. Ran. In boots. The cabs weren't running and I don't own a car. He was worried sick." She thought it best not to bring up being stopped by the police. Simon really could use a lesson or two in diplomacy. She'd known as sure as rain that he was about to mouth off at that cop, and the only place that would get them was possibly arrested. The only place worse than her apartment to be in a blackout.

"Oh. He didn't say."

Charles Thackeray struck her as an academic who immersed himself in other times and places and didn't invest much in the here and now.

"No. He wouldn't, would he?" she countered.

"No, I don't suppose he would. Always been a bit of a loner, our boy. And a little standoffish."

Tawny managed not to gape and literally bit her tongue to keep from mouthing off about the pot calling the kettle black and the apple not falling far from the tree. Instead she contented herself with saying, "You just have to work a little harder to get to know him, but he's definitely worth the effort."

He looked at her as if she'd just expostulated a new scientific hypothesis but didn't comment.

"So it was definitely a heart attack?" she asked.

"Yes. Chest pains woke her around midnight. Letitia's one of the most sensible women I know. She didn't know if it was the heat, indigestion or a heart attack. Instead of ignoring it, she told me to bring her to the hospital. Said she'd rather be embarrassed if it was indigestion than dead if it wasn't. Very sensible woman."

"I've seen the statistics. A frightening number of women die unnecessarily each year from heart attacks because they wait too long to seek treatment or simply ignore the symptoms," Tawny said.

Apparently Charles Thackeray wasn't as together as he seemed. Tears welled in his eyes. *Great, Tawny. Make him cry by driving home how close his wife had come to dying.* She awkwardly patted his arm.

"I'm glad she's fine now."

Charles nodded. "Something in my eye. Yes, of course. Good thing she's such a sensible woman. Let's go in so she can meet you."

Tawny thought that since she'd opened her big mouth about dying that he really just needed to reassure himself that his wife was, indeed, okay.

"I'll just wait out here till Simon's through visiting with her."

"Nonsense. Simon will want to know you're here and I'm sure Letitia will want to meet you."

Short of making a big stink, which didn't seem the thing to do, Tawny had little choice but to allow him to usher her into the room ahead of him.

In a quick glance Tawny took in the situation. Simon stood to the right of the hospital bed, looking terribly uncomfortable and self-conscious. She checked out his mother.

She'd mentally prepared herself for a Gorgonesque creature. She was quite surprised at how… well, *normal* the woman in bed looked, even though she was hooked up to the telemetry machine. A chin-length bob of dark hair shot through with silver framed an angular, wan face and eyes the shape and color of Simon's.

"Letty, this is Tawny Edwards." He paused significantly and then continued, "She's here with Simon."

Without thinking, Tawny moved to stand beside Simon and took his hand in hers, more for her benefit than his. She didn't know why she was suffering this sudden attack of nerves.

"I'm so pleased to meet you." Letitia Thackeray's crisp British accent was far more pronounced than her husband's.

"It's nice to meet you, as well—" Tawny paused to smile "—although I wish it were under better circumstances." She shifted self-consciously. Her Southern accent came across as thick as molasses in contrast to Letitia's clipped tone. "How are you feeling?"

"I'm fine. A little glitch in the system, but I'm going to be right as rain." She looked from Tawny to Simon and back again.

Charles smiled at his wife. The tenderness that passed between them nearly took Tawny's breath. Charles nodded. "It's that way."

"What way?" Simon asked. No one answered him. Tawny had no idea what Charles was talking about either. It was as if Charles and Letitia shared their own language.

"Oh, wonderful." Letitia beamed at Tawny from her pillow. "Simon's never brought a girl home to meet us before."

Home to meet them? News flash: they weren't exactly sitting in a drawing room sipping tea and munching crumpets. And they'd totally misinterpreted her and Simon's relationship. Heck, she and Simon didn't *have* a relationship. Talk about a wrong impression. She tried to let go of Simon's hand.

"But—"

Instead of releasing her hand, Simon squeezed it and glanced at the monitor beeping by his mother's bed. All righty, then. For right now they had a relationship. And it was whatever his mother wanted it to be.

Tawny smiled at the bedridden woman and hoped her smile wasn't as weak as it felt. "Yes…well, I wish I was meeting you both under different circumstances."

"No, dear girl." This was moving fast—she was already a *dear girl*. "This is wonderful." Letitia lowered her voice and took on a confiding tone. "Charles and I had begun to worry that he might be a bit of a poofter. You know, gay."

This family had some serious communication issues.

Simon uttered a choking noise and his ears turned bright red. "Mum…"

"He's definitely not," Tawny blurted without thinking. *Oh, crud.* She shouldn't have said *that* in such a knowing tone. Not to his *parents.* She, Tawny Marianne Edwards, was zipping her lip until they got out of here. She wasn't saying another word.

Far from offended, they seemed pleased by her outburst. Charles winked at Letitia. "See, I told you it was that way."

Tawny glanced at Simon. She saw the kindness and integrity in his brown eyes, the endearing tinge of red still burning his ears. She curled her fingers around his, his grip firm and sure. Her heart flip-flopped queerly as she realized that it was, indeed, that way.

"SIMON AND TAWNY RAN SIX miles to get here, Letty. And Simon's wearing boots," his dad said with a touch of awe and pride.

"You ran to see me?" his mother asked, a hint of wonder reflected in both her voice and her eyes.

Simon knew he was wading deeper into muck, but he'd sort it out when his mother wasn't lying in a hospital bed connected to monitors with an oxygen tube clipped to her nose. She'd looked so bloody pleased— they both had—when they'd misconstrued his and Tawny's relationship. And then when Tawny had looked at him as if she was somewhere beyond besotted…

"Well, not quite six miles. We managed a lift the last bit."

"In boots?"

He would've never guessed that he was this important to them. Emotion clogged his throat.

"I needed to make sure you were okay." It came out brusque and clipped.

His mother didn't seem to mind. "That's wonderful."

"He's a wonderful man. You should spend some time getting to know him," Tawny said. Despite her soft voice, her look challenged both of his parents.

Her statement hung in the air, the bleep of the telemetry the only sound in the room. His dad stood a little straighter, his mouth pinched. No one took Charles Thackeray or Letitia Marbury to task. Simon nearly gaped when his father's face softened and he took his wife's hand in his.

"Perhaps you're right, young lady. I suspect our son is rather wonderful."

It was as close as his family had ever come to a Hallmark moment. And probably ever would. Simon was bloody close to blubbering.

It was just as well that Elliott breezed through the door, shattering the moment. "Dr. M, what are you doing here?"

What was Elliott doing here? Elliott brushed past them to hug Simon's mother. In the meantime, Simon glanced at Tawny and murmured, "You did this?"

She looked guilty but unrepentant. "I didn't know what you'd be faced with. I thought you might need him," she said quietly in his ear, leaning in under the guise of brushing something off of his shirt.

Elliott straightened and threw an arm around Simon's shoulders. "Simon. Thanks for taking care of my girl."

"Your girl? We thought..." His mother trailed off, frowning in confusion.

Elliott offered a charming smile. "Sure. Tawny and I are engaged. Didn't Simon tell you?"

"No. That particular detail wasn't mentioned." His father's eyebrows beetled together into a unibrow.

"But Simon and Tawny..." His mother verged on tears.

"Elliott's such a kidder." Tawny swatted at Elliott, angled so that only Elliott and Simon saw the serious glint in her eyes. "Quit teasing Dr. Marbury." She looked back at his mother. "We need to let you get some rest. In fact, come on guys, we'll go get a coffee." She stopped just short of snapping her fingers at them.

His mother beamed her approval. "Ah, a woman after my own heart, one who knows how to take charge." She nodded at Simon. "You've done well, son. I like her."

"I like her, as well," his father said.

Well, bully, they were three for three, because so

did he. This would be a fine mess to sort out later. "I'm a lucky guy."

"I'm the lucky one," Tawny said, casting an adoring look his way.

"But…" Elliott looked from one to the other, clearly confused.

Tawny cut him off. "An iced coffee would be heaven, wouldn't it? Let's go find the café." She grabbed Elliott by the arm.

"Ouch. You pinched me," he said.

"Oops. Sorry about that." She turned to Simon's mother. "Try to get some rest."

"I will. Thank you for coming with Simon." His mother looked at him. "You will stop back in before you leave, won't you?"

"Yes. Get some sleep."

Tawny led Elliott from the room. Simon followed. Tawny in charge was a formidable sight.

They'd barely made it to the hall when Elliott said, "What was that—"

"Put a lid on it, Elliott," Tawny snapped at him. "I desperately need a cup of coffee to make me close to human. We'll talk then."

She swept forward like a regal queen. Elliott deserved everything and anything she threw his way, and Simon was damned glad he wasn't Elliott.

Richard straightened from where he'd been leaning against the wall across from the nurses' station and approached Elliott. The look that passed between them was the unmistakable look shared by lovers.

"I see you *did* bring the rainbow coalition," Tawny said.

Richard glared at Tawny and linked his arm through Elliott's.

Simon found it fairly disconcerting to see his best friend arm in arm with his gay lover. But in the scheme of things, no more disconcerting than finding himself in Tawny's bed or discovering that his parents thought he might be gay. Altogether it had been a very curious night. And it wasn't over yet.

They took the next available elevator. At half past three in the morning they were the only passengers.

The doors closed and Elliott drew a deep breath, sniffing the air like a scent hound. He visibly paled, looking askance at first Tawny and then Simon.

"The two of you slept together." It wasn't a question.

"What are you talking about?" Tawny challenged.

"The two of you...you reek of sex." Elliott rounded on Simon. "I can't believe you screwed my fiancée."

Simon had known they'd have this conversation one day, he just hadn't anticipated it being quite so soon. He looked pointedly at Richard. "You don't have a lot of room for outrage."

Tawny moved to stand directly in front of Elliott, her body screaming confrontation.

"Let's get a couple of things straight. I'm not your fiancée. Who I screw, when I screw and how I screw is no longer any of your business. I could do the entire NY Giants team for halftime entertainment and it wouldn't be any of your business. Once you dipped your wick there—" she stabbed a finger in Richard's general direction "—you were never coming here again. Literally or figuratively."

"Honey, his wick's no longer interested in anything you've got," Richard sniped.

"Which is a good thing," she lobbed back.

Simon bit back a laugh. Well said. She'd bloody well laid it all on the line. She really was a magnificent woman.

The doors opened to the first floor and Simon herded everyone off the elevator.

"I think we could all use a cup of tea…or coffee," he said, steering everyone to the right, following the signs to the café.

Tawny grumbled at Elliott. "You were supposed to show up to support Simon, not act like a jerk."

"Well, I guess if Simon doesn't like it you can always kiss it and make it better," Elliott said with a sneer.

Simon had a fairly good idea of how much will power Tawny employed to ignore Elliott's comment. Doubtless, flaunting her and Simon's night in Elliott's face was tempting, especially considering Elliott had brought his new lover along. But apparently she'd been sincere when she'd said she hadn't slept with him to get back at Elliott. Instead she ignored his jibe.

"How did you get here so quick?" she said.

"There's no way you got here in that amount of time from the gallery."

"My apartment's only a couple of blocks away," Richard said, letting the cat out of the bag.

Simon felt sucker-punched. Certainly he was a sucker. Elliott hadn't been locked in at the gallery. He'd used him. Lied to him and used him. Their friendship had weathered the occasional row, but never would he have believed Elliott would lie to him. He stopped outside of the café entrance, restraining Elliott with a hand on his arm.

"Thanks, Richard. I'd love for you to buy me a cup of coffee," Tawny said, very much tongue in cheek but obviously trying to get Richard to give Elliott and Simon a moment of privacy.

Elliott glanced at Richard. "Please. Do it for me."

"Well, since it's for you," Richard said, giving Tawny a look of distaste. He reluctantly followed her into the café.

"Were you *ever* locked in at the gallery?" Simon asked with quiet fury.

"Yes. It does go into lockdown mode."

"For how long?" Simon's anger rendered him nearly speechless.

Elliott shoved his hands into his pockets and looked abashed. "About an hour. The security system people talked me through disarming it."

"Was this before or after you asked me to break your news to Tawny?"

"After. Definitely after. I swear to you, Simon."

He felt marginally better—*if* Elliott wasn't lying. For fifteen years they'd been as close as brothers, and in less than a day he no longer knew if he could trust Elliott. He no longer knew the man before him. The man he'd loved like a brother couldn't have betrayed his fiancée, wouldn't have left Simon to clean up his mess. "Yet when you got out of the gallery, you didn't think you needed to come over to Tawny's?"

"You were already taking care of it. I thought it would be best to let her sleep on it. I didn't know she'd be sleeping on it with you."

Simon's anger dissipated as quickly as it had swamped him, leaving exhaustion in its wake. He hadn't used Elliott, but he had betrayed him to some extent. Simon realized he'd come across as something of a sanctimonious bastard. Two women in scrubs walked past and he waited until they were out of earshot.

"Elliott, you put both of us in that position. Do you know she's afraid of the dark?"

"Of course I do. We were together for six months."

"Then why did you tell me to leave her there alone? That struck me as rather callous."

Elliott shoved his hands into his trouser pockets and avoided Simon's eyes. "Things have already been a bit rocky between us. I told you we haven't been setting any records in the bedroom—" Right, and Tawny'd pretty much said the same. "She says I whine and that I'm self-centered."

"You do and you are."

Elliott looked at him then. "I might a tad, but she's so damned bossy."

"She is." Simon considered it part of her charm. It rather naturally came with the territory. She was also smart and gutsy and brave as hell. He thought about walking down those seven flights of stairs without even a candle. He didn't harbor any fears of the dark and it had been rather creepy for him. But Elliott still hadn't gotten to the point. "And what's that got to do with you asking me to abandon her in the dark?"

"I don't know. I knew things weren't good between us, but I didn't want to think about her being alone with another man, even if it was you."

"A case of wanting your cake and eating it, as well?"

"I'm a self-serving bastard," Elliott said.

"In a nutshell, yes."

"You didn't have to agree with me so quickly."

"You merely said it before I could," Simon said.

"I think I went a little crazy tonight."

"Are you rethinking your decisions?" Simon asked.

"Not Richard and Tawny. I just regret the way I've handled it all. I made some very bad decisions tonight and I'm not sure how to fix this. I'm afraid I've jeopardized our friendship." It was more question than statement.

"You didn't ax-murder any little old ladies, did you?"

"Not that I recall."

"I think we're okay then. Tonight…with Tawny… We didn't mean for it to happen. And if it hurt you…well, I'm sorry for that."

Elliott rested his head in his hands. He shook his head, as if to clear it. He looked at Simon in evident remorse.

"Simon, I don't deserve a friend like you."

"True enough."

"Would you let me self-flagellate without interrupting?"

"I'll try."

"I was being a jealous bitch. I knew once Tawny found out about Richard it would be over between us. I know her well enough to know that. But when I walked in and your arm was around her and…well, I know for a fact she never looked at me the way she looks at you."

Simon shook his head. It was late, everyone was tired and edgy. "That was for my mother's benefit. She and my father leaped to the wrong conclusion and I thought under the circumstances it was best to let Mum think what she wanted."

"How'd you know she was at the hospital?"

"Dad called."

The surprise on Elliott's face said it all. Simon laughed. "I know."

"You okay?"

"I'm fine. Sort of." He shook his head. "Tawny

told them they ought to spend some time getting to know me."

"No kidding? What'd your father do?"

"I thought he'd go off, but he and Mum said they thought she was right or some other bit of rubbish."

"Maybe they're changing, Simon. It's about damn time."

"Well, it doesn't make any sense. I'm still the same person I've always been."

"See, that's where you're wrong, where you've always been wrong. I've been telling you for years…you think you've been the problem. Whether you're the same person or not is immaterial, because it's always been about them. They were the ones with the problem, not you. Tawny read them the riot act." Elliott laughed. "I'm sorry I missed that part. I told you, Tawny's a steel magnolia."

"She is a bit relentless. She said her nickname growing up was Bulldog."

"I can believe it. There's another thing you've got wrong, Simon. I know Tawny. She's not an actress. She wears her feelings on her sleeve. The way she was looking at you wasn't for your mother's benefit."

Elliott himself had said his judgment was skewed tonight. "You're wrong."

"Simon, we've known each other for a long time and you don't know how relieved I am that I haven't totally botched our friendship."

"I feel a *but* coming and I've got an inkling I'm not going to particularly like it."

"Probably not. For the life of me, I can't figure out why you're so damned scared of being happy."

11

TAWNY NURSED AN ICED coffee that tasted like chilled sewer water—at least, what she thought sewer water would taste like—and ignored Richard two tables over. She wasn't pining over Elliott, but she wasn't quite prepared to embrace the new object of his desire. She was glad Elliott and Simon had stayed outside the café to talk. She needed a few minutes alone to sort out her head.

She wasn't sure whether to laugh or cry. She was in love with Simon. Somewhere between "Elliott's seeing someone else" and "It's that way between them" she'd fallen head over heels in love with him.

Damn if she hadn't gotten exactly what she'd wanted—a stiletto kind of love. There was nothing old-shoe comfortable about Simon. He was alternately caustic and tender and brave and vulnerable. She knew with a certainty that almost frightened her in its intensity that whether it was a year from now or twenty years from now or fifty, she'd still feel the same.

Maybe this had started when they'd spent the day together shooting the pictures for Elliott, and her erotic dreams had been trying to tell her what her head and heart weren't ready to hear.

Lost in thought, Elliott startled her when he dropped into the chair next to her. "Simon says we need to talk."

She had it bad, in a major kind of way. A thrill coursed through her at the mere mention of his name. Elliott, however, remained at the top of her jerk list. "So talk."

"I'm sorry," he said.

He should be. "I agree. You're a sorry excuse for a human being. You not only cheated on me but you lied to me tonight when I called you about Simon's mother. You deliberately let me think you were still locked in at the gallery."

"I know. It was wrong. You can't call me anything I haven't already called myself. I knew you'd be angry and if Simon found out so would he. I just didn't want to face it tonight. I didn't want to deal with it."

"You created the monster, Dr. Frankenstein. Deal with it."

"You're right."

"I am." How could you continue to berate someone who simply agreed with you? What she'd really wanted to say to him when she saw him face-to-face was that she hoped his dick would drop off, but now…he'd probably just agree with her, and where was the satisfaction in that?

"I'm sorry for so many things...for not having the courage to tell you how conflicted I was about my sexuality before things went further with Richard. Then I should've been man enough to face you alone and tell you myself. And I'm sorry for being a jerk earlier."

She'd never been a grudge holder. She forgave far too easily. She wasn't sure whether she was cursed or blessed. And her ability to so easily forgive his betrayal also spoke to the fact that she hadn't loved him the way she should love a man to marry him. And despite the fact that her logic and rationale had been impugned tonight, she was a very logical woman. If Elliott hadn't behaved the way he had at every turn, tonight might never have happened with Simon. And she was immensely, intensely glad that tonight had happened with Simon. She had no regrets.

"That about covers it with us. I accept your apology and I no longer hope that your dick drops off."

Surprise, followed closely by relief, chased across his face. He chuckled. "I didn't want you pissed at me forever."

"I can't say I particularly like Richard, but if you care about him and he makes you happy, then I'm happy for you."

"Thank you. That's more than I deserve."

"Yeah, it is, isn't it?" Tawny grinned and Elliott reached over and smoothed her hair behind her ear.

"You're a kick-ass woman, Tawny. A part of me wishes things had worked out with us."

"It never would have, Elliott. And I have to say I'm glad it didn't," she said. "I'm okay, but have you made things right with Simon?"

Elliott nodded. "We're good. We talked about what happened earlier." He grimaced. "I've had to eat a lot of humble pie tonight."

"Only your fair share."

"Could you maybe go a little easy on me?"

"I'm not sure you deserve it, but I'll try."

"We talked about his parents."

"It's odd. I thoroughly detested them for the way they've treated him, but I couldn't help but like them when I met them."

"Welcome to my world. They've totally screwed up Simon's head—and it's a mess—but they're not deliberately cruel, just thoughtless. They've always been courteous. I never felt unwelcome in their house when we were teenagers, but there's always this distance. Fine if you're the friend, but it really sucks if you're their kid. Simon pretends it doesn't matter, pretends he doesn't care, but all he's ever wanted was for them to notice him." He looked thoroughly disgusted. "They didn't even make it to our high school graduation."

Tawny ached on Simon's behalf and thought more of him than ever before. "He didn't hesitate when his dad called and asked him to come. And from the sound of things, that's so much more than they deserved. He deserves better parents."

Elliott smiled faintly at her vehemence. "A lot of people do. But we have to play the hand we're dealt. Simon's one of the finest men I know, but they've scarred him."

She drew a deep breath and plunged into the deep end with both feet. "I love him, Elliott." It felt new and fresh and all the more real for giving it voice. Even now she was aware of him across the room with every fiber of her being.

The melancholy in Elliot's eyes touched her. He nodded. "I know."

"You do? How could you possibly…?"

"I knew the second I saw the two of you together in Dr. M's room." Elliott creased the napkin on the table between them.

She laughed self-consciously. "Ridiculous, isn't it? Yesterday you and I were engaged and now I'm sitting here telling you I'm in love with him."

"I wouldn't say it's ridiculous at all. I'd say it's just the way it is, much the same as me winding up with Richard."

"You're his best friend. I need you to be okay with this." It wasn't particularly easy asking for his blessing.

"I have to be okay with it, otherwise you'll nag me to death *and* kick my ass in the meantime."

They both laughed. Elliott sobered.

"You'll have to fight for him, Tawny."

Her gut knotted. "I know he's in love with someone else…or at least he thinks he is. Who is she?"

"I know there is someone—someone he won't discuss, which isn't unusual for Simon because he's very self-contained. But that's not who I'm talking about." His blue eyes held a trace of pity. "It's Simon you'll have to fight."

"I HOPED I'D FIND YOU HERE. She's asleep."

Startled, Simon looked up from adding sugar to his coffee. It was time lapse at its worst—his father had aged ten years in the span of a night. Talking to his father was always more awkward than conversing with a stranger.

"Can I buy you a cup?" Simon offered.

"Any chance of scaring up a cup of tea?"

"Find us a table and I'll see what I can do," he said.

In record time he returned with a steaming cup of water, a tea bag, cream and sugar. "It's the best I could do."

The table rocked when he sat down.

"Thank you. I seem to have found the one with the wobble."

"It's fine," Simon said. He didn't think they'd be here long enough for it to matter.

His father set the tea to steeping and an awkward silence settled between them, the same general stiffness he'd felt his whole life with his parents.

Simon cleared his throat. "Since Mum's fine and she's resting, we won't go back up. You'll explain it to her, won't you? Tell her I didn't want to wake her?"

His father nodded his gray head. "I'll let her know. Thank you for coming."

Had he doubted that Simon would? "Anytime. I'm glad you called me."

Silence stretched between them like a thin, taut trip wire. His father, with neat precise movements, prepared his tea. One sugar. A dollop of cream. No lemon. Stir twice. As a child, his father's tea-making ritual had fascinated him in its unswerving sameness.

Charles looked up from his cup, catching Simon unaware. "She wanted you here…and so did I."

"All you had to do was call." Perhaps it was exhaustion. Perhaps it was the courage to say things in the wee hours of the morning. But Simon said, "All I ever wanted was for you to love me."

His father's ever-erect carriage faltered. He looked like a tired old man. He shook his head. "I fear we've been terrible parents. I've always loved your mother so much, I didn't make room for anyone else. That was wrong, dreadfully wrong. When I thought I might lose her tonight, I realized how important not just she is to me but you, as well. To both of us. I believe Tawny was right, we've got a wonderful son we need to get to know."

The chill inside him had nothing to do with the air-conditioning. "I don't want to be the putty that fills the gap just because you think you might lose her."

"No. Never that. Your mother and I have missed you these last couple of years. But things have come full circle. Whether it was your intention or not, you cut us out of your life."

There was nothing to say, so Simon remained silent.

His father nodded in acknowledgment. "It was nothing more than we deserved. We can't change the past. All we have is the future. Your mother and I would like to be a part of your life."

He'd waited a lifetime for this. He should be ecstatic. But he'd built a wall around his emotions. Every hurt, every lonely hour had mortared yet another brick into place. One offer of intent couldn't tear down something so firmly in place. Simon rubbed at his neck, stiff with tension. "I don't know."

"Fair enough."

Charles sipped his tea. Simon finished his coffee. His father cleared his throat.

"Well, yes. What about Tawny? *Is* she Elliott's fiancée?"

Simon infinitely preferred to focus on Tawny and Elliott instead of his relationship or lack thereof with his parents. "Up until last evening she was Elliott's fiancée. I'm not gay and never will be. Elliot however, just came out of the closet."

His father blinked. Twice. "This is rather akin to a racy BBC drama."

Simon smiled. His father never meant to be funny, but sometimes…well, he just was. Simon shook his head. "It gets rather complicated, but the bottom line is Tawny and I aren't an item. I got stuck at her apartment last night—well, this evening—and when Mum thought that…well, we just let her think it."

"Ah, that's just details and I really don't need to know all of that. All I need to know is the look on your face when she came through the door." He wrapped his hands around the cup and Simon noted the prominent blue veins that came with aging. "You and she share the same thing your mother and I have always shared. A current that runs deep, a connection few others get."

He'd explained they didn't have a relationship, but he bloody well had no intention of discussing his *feelings* with this man who'd never evinced the slightest interest in his feelings before.

"Wouldn't you say it's a bit late in the day to decide you're interested in my life?"

"That's ultimately up to you, but no, I don't. I can't change yesterday, but I can change tomorrow."

Simon didn't know what to say. He wouldn't promise anything he couldn't deliver on and he just didn't know if it was too little, too late.

His father looked disappointed. "Okay. Will you come back tomorrow, or rather later today, to see your mother?"

"I'll come back."

It was the most he could promise.

"YOU MUST BE LIVING RIGHT. What are the odds of finding a parking spot on a Manhattan street?" Tawny said as Simon eased his father's aged Jaguar into an empty space within half a block of her building.

"Must be all the poor sods stuck at work," he said with a slight smile.

Charles Thackeray had offered his car since he wasn't going anywhere and Simon would be returning in the morning…well, later today. She'd been more than content to ride home in air-conditioning as opposed to running. They'd driven the dark streets in companionable silence, each wrapped in their own thoughts.

"Dad said there's a flashlight in the trunk. Give me a minute to get it," Simon said, opening his door and getting out.

Fine by her. The worn leather seats were soft like a glove. It was no hardship to sit on her butt a little longer.

The trunk slammed and Simon appeared at her door, flashlight in hand, the beam of light making the surrounding dark all the thicker. He opened the door for her. "At least we don't have to tackle the stairs in the dark this time."

"I'm eternally grateful to your father," she said, climbing out of the car, Simon's hand beneath her elbow. He was a thoroughly modern man with an endearingly old-fashioned sense of gallantry.

The street lay quiet, deserted. She and Simon seemed to be the only two people awake in the city. Even the few voices they'd heard when they'd left earlier were now silent.

They walked to the front of her building. "It was nice to drive."

His teeth flashed white in a weary grin. "It did beat the hell out of walking back."

Once in the front door, Simon took her hand in his as they followed the swath of light across the lobby to the stairwell.

"I'm not so sure that dad would've offered the Jag if it had been only me. I bet you've never met anyone that didn't like you," he said as they climbed the stairs.

Tawny felt sure he was talking to distract her from the dark. Even with the flashlight the inky black played host to her worst fears. She focused on the conversation and tried not to think about being swallowed up by the dark.

"That's not true. For the most part I get along with everyone. I like people. I think that's why it bothered me so much that you seemed to dislike me from the moment you met me."

"I've never disliked you."

She snorted but didn't argue the point. "And Mrs. Hinky doesn't like me."

"Mrs. Hinky?"

"My next door neighbor. But she doesn't like anyone. Personally I think she's a bit of a nutcase, sort of paranoid. She's convinced people spy on her."

Simon made a choking noise. "Does she live to your right, if you're facing your building?"

"Yeah." How did Simon know Mrs. Hinky?

Simon recounted his earlier impromptu flashing on the ledge. Tawny laughed until she was gasping for air.

"Oh my God. That would've totally freaked out anyone, but especially Mrs. Hinky…." She dissolved into more laughter.

"Poor woman. I'm sure I was her worst nightmare come to life."

"I've seen you naked and it's no nightmare. But I'd better go over and explain tomorrow—well, later today—just so she's not totally freaked out."

"Probably not a bad idea." He tugged on her hand to stop her. "We're here."

It hadn't taken them any time. "You sure?"

"Yep." He flashed the beam onto the number stenciled on the door. "Seventh floor."

They were quiet walking down the dark hall. Reaching her apartment, Tawny unlocked the door and they stepped inside. Inside it was as hot now as it had been when they'd left.

"Hold on a sec and I'll have this lit," Simon said. A small votive flickered to life. He turned off the flashlight. "Don't want to run the batteries down."

With a meow, Simon, née Peaches, greeted her. Amazed, she scooped him up.

"Hey. Did you miss us?" She glanced over at Simon, who now had two pillar candles lit. "Wow. He's never greeted me before."

The cat batted at her chin with his clawless paw. She laughed and put him back down. "Okay. Enough already, huh?"

"It's the name change," Simon said, a ghost of a smile hovering around his mouth.

"Maybe. Or it could be my faith that he'd come around one day. Our perceptions become our reality." Wow. Where had that come from? She must be tired if she was spewing philosophical sound bites.

Exhaustion rooted her to the spot. Physically, emotionally, mentally, she was spent. She stretched and caught a whiff of her underarm. Ew.

"I could sleep a week, but I've got to shower first. Want to hop in with me? Just to shower," she tacked on, making sure he knew she wasn't offering sex.

"Sure." Simon laughed. "I'm not capable of anything more right now. I don't think I could get it up. Not even for you."

She smiled. That was one of the things she loved about Simon. He was so real. How many guys would admit that? She skirted the couch. "Good. I couldn't do more than lay there and I'd probably fall asleep, even if you could get it up."

He slipped his arm around her waist and she welcomed the support. "Okay then. Shower only."

Votive in one hand, the other arm wrapped around her, he ushered her down the hall and into the bathroom. He put the candle on the sink, the mirror reflecting the light.

Tawny toed off her shoes and skimmed out of her shorts, panties and socks. Her top and bra joined the heap of dirty clothes on the floor.

She watched as Simon finished undressing— boots and jeans took a little longer to shuck. Absolutely lovely. Lean and muscular. He looked up and caught her watching him.

"What?"

"I'm tired, Simon, not unconscious. I'm just taking a moment to enjoy the view."

He grinned at her and walked over to turn on the shower. Those shoulders, trim waist, tight butt, muscular thighs. Arousal fluttered low in her belly. She felt the instant rush of desire that translated to slick, wet heat between her thighs.

"If I wasn't so beat, I'd try to seduce you into sweaty, nasty, on-the-floor, banging-my-head-against-the-wall sex," she said.

He quirked an eyebrow at her over his shoulder and she laughed softly. His expression was part hopeful and part weary disbelief. She shook her head. "It's a shame to waste the moment when you're all naked and—" she eyed his tight, bare buns "—well, naked. But I'm just too tired."

He laughed and stepped over his piled clothes to take her hand. "I may have to burn these clothes when I get home."

He led her to the shower. She didn't want to think about him going home. She didn't want the magic of

the night to end. "I don't know about burning them…
maybe just a fumigation."

She stepped beneath the shower's icy spray. The
cold water felt delicious against her sticky, sweaty
skin. An easy silence encompassed them as she and
Simon alternated turns beneath the spray. When she'd
shampooed and scrubbed every inch of herself and
Simon had done the same, she turned the water off.

She swayed on her feet. Now clean and cool, she
gave in to the fatigue weighing her limbs and numb-
ing her mind.

"Hold on." Simon grabbed her towel off the hook
and gently began to dry her.

"I can do that," she protested, but she made no
move to take the towel from him.

"Of course you can," he agreed. He reached
around her and blotted the water from her back. She
gave into temptation and rested her head against his
strong shoulder.

"Hold on just a little bit longer," he said. He
straightened and toweled her arms, chest and belly.

She stared, fascinated by the water clinging to his
dark lashes and the drops caught in the stubble dark-
ening his jaw.

"Mmm." It was nice to be coddled. "Believe it or
not, I require more than an hour of sleep."

Simon chuckled as he knelt to dry her legs. The
faint candlelight danced along the ripple of muscles
in his shoulders, reflected off the sheen of moisture

along the lean line of his back. He straightened, draped the towel over her wet hair and started doing some wonderful massage thing to her head. She groaned aloud.

"You've got to stop doing that or I'm going to fall asleep standing up."

He settled the towel around her shoulders and grinned. "That wouldn't be good."

He grabbed the other towel and made quick work of drying himself off while she stood there and watched like zombie-girl in la-la land. Simon stepped out of the tub. Before she knew what he was about, he placed one arm behind her shoulders, the other beneath her knees and scooped her up. His bare skin was cool and clean next to hers.

She should protest. Too heavy. Not necessary. But exhaustion muted her. Instead she linked her arms around his neck and pillowed her cheek against his chest, inhaling the scent of soap and Simon. The steady rhythm of his heart played like a lullaby beneath her cheek. Supported by his arms, his skin against hers, surrounded by his scent, she gave herself over to sleep….

12

Simon watched Tawny sleep, the sun slanting across her buttocks and legs, her arm flung over her face, her hair an auburn skein across her pillow.

He rolled out of bed and padded into the bathroom. He pulled on his underwear and jeans. Walking around naked last night had been one thing but quite another this morning. The night's magic had vanished with the dawn.

He retrieved his camera and adjusted for the bright light streaming into the room. Neither of them had thought to pull the blinds when they'd stumbled into bed four short hours ago. She lay partially illuminated and partially in shadow. He took several photos, caught up in the play of sunlight over her skin. Retreating once again behind the safety of his camera.

She blinked her eyes open and smiled sleepily at him, and his pulse quickened. She eyed his camera. "Please tell me you aren't taking photos of me with bed head and no makeup."

She was a quixotic woman—undeterred by her

nudity but worried about her lack of makeup. "You look beautiful," he said without thinking. And she did, with her hair tangled about her shoulders and her eyes soft and heavy-lidded with sleep.

"Right." She held a hand up between herself and the camera. "No more early-morning shots. Please."

"Okay." She did truly look beautiful, but she'd be self-conscious now. He walked over to the window and looked out at the city, offering her a moment of privacy without actually leaving the room.

The mattress creaked, announcing she was up. He heard her pad out of the room and the protesting squawk of the bathroom door.

Once again people crowded the street below, but very few cars were about. He fired off a few shots without any real interest. His heart wasn't in photographing the scene before him.

He heard the door squawk again and she walked back into the room.

"Thanks for going with me to the hospital last night," he said without turning around. They'd both been too tired to talk through anything earlier.

She opened and closed a dresser drawer. "I'm glad I got to meet your parents. What a relief your mom's okay."

"Yeah. It is." Simon winced inside. This was a bad case of *morning-afteritis*. They both sounded like characters in a poorly scripted play.

"I liked them better than I thought I would," she said, her voice muffled by the closet.

"They were…different." And that was an understatement. It was so typical that their decision to participate in his life revolved around their needs. They hadn't reached out to him because they were proud of him, or because they'd realized they'd missed out on knowing a great human being. No. They were feeling their mortality, their vulnerability, so he was their backup. Simon still played second fiddle to their agenda. And he didn't trust any of it. Now that his mum was fine, he fully expected they'd return to their insular world of two. "They certainly liked you."

"I tried not to be too unleashed for them." She peered around him to the street below.

Her hair brushed against his arm, her scent surrounded him and the urge to take her in his arms was almost unbearable, but the night's madness had ended.

"You charmed them," he said, stepping back from the window, away from her.

"Hah! They would've been thrilled with anyone who would've saved you from being—what was it?—a poofter."

Despite the heaviness of his heart and the general awkwardness dancing between them, Simon laughed. "Right. That was rich, wasn't it? If I've never brought a woman to meet them, therefore I must be gay. Face it, Tawny, you charm everyone."

"Hah! Don't forget about Mrs. Hinky. And I can guarantee you I didn't charm Richard."

"You and Richard got off to a less than stellar start." Bloody understatement. "You're square with Elliott?" Simon asked. He needed to make sure before he left.

"We're good. I've got closure, so I can forego the Prozac," she said, smiling. "And you guys kissed and made up?"

Simon shrugged. "We skipped the kiss—I didn't fancy Richard scratching my eyes out—but we're okay." He was making stupid, awkward jokes—definitely time for him to leave. He started toward the door and she stepped in front of him, stopping him.

She placed her hands on his bare chest, and his skin felt on fire. She wet her lips with the tip of her tongue. "Simon, I want you to know last night was the best night of my life."

He stepped back, away from her touch. "That's an unusual reaction to a broken engagement."

She dropped her hands to her side. Her look chastised him. "That's not what I meant and you know it. *You* were the best part of last night."

"I'm flattered." And he was, but one of them had to be sensible. He walked out of the room. His camera case was still by the front door. It wasn't the pitch-black of last night, but a dark gloom curtained the room after the bright sunlight of the bedroom.

Undeterred, she followed him. "I'm not trying to flatter you. I'm being honest. Remember last night, when your father told your mother it was 'like that' between the two of us?"

He picked up his camera case without looking at her. "Yes. And I'm sorry that happened. I didn't want to upset her when she'd had a heart attack."

"I'm not sorry it happened. When he said that, well, I realized he had half of it right."

He snapped his head up. Had she guessed he was head over heels in love with her? "What do you mean?"

"I realized it is that way for me," she said, her voice soft in the shadowed room.

Simon clamped down on the ache inside him. She'd been raw and vulnerable last night. She'd very likely feel the same about any other guy who'd stepped in and treated her with any measure of decency. "No, Tawny, last night was extenuating circumstances. You were emotionally overwrought. Don't confuse the circumstances of the night with me."

"Are you implying I don't know how I feel?" This time her soft tone heralded an impending storm. But what he had to say needed to be said.

He'd already taken advantage of her to some extent last night. He'd be a total jerk to let her run with this now. And if he told her how he felt about her? Tomorrow or next week or perhaps next month, she'd realize how flawed he was, she'd see the darkness in him and he'd see the loathing in her eyes. It was far better this way.

"Last night was an emotional roller coaster for

you. Give it a couple of days and it'll just be the night the lights went out in the big city."

"Don't you dare patronize me."

"I'm just being rational. One of us has to be." He knew the instant it left his mouth *that* was the wrong thing to say.

"Tell me I did not just hear you say that, Simon Thackeray."

He simply wanted her to see what was painfully apparent to him. Last night had been a space out of time. If she'd just be rational, she'd see that today it was back to the norm. But then again, maybe she couldn't be right now. Maybe it was that hormonally challenged time of the month.

"Are you maybe getting ready to start?"

"To start what?"

"You know…are you PMSing?" he asked.

The cat yowled from the other room.

"Luckily for you, I'm not. If I were, you'd probably be a dead man by now." She stomped into the kitchen. He heard her shaking cat food into the bowl as he walked past. He picked up his shirt, socks and boots. He pulled on his shirt. He sat on the edge of the sofa to put on his socks and boots. She came back out of the kitchen and lit a couple of candles without speaking.

"Listen, it's no wonder you're not thinking clearly, with Elliott coming out of the closet, the blackout, being dragged out to the hospital in the middle of the night. It's hotter than hell and you haven't had much sleep," he said, lacing his boot.

"That may all be well and true, but I have enough God-given sense to know how I feel."

"You'll see everything differently once the power's back on. A cool room, a hot shower, a decent meal and a good night's rest will make a world of difference."

She planted her hands on her hips, the heat and her temper obviously getting the best of her. "All the electricity in the world isn't going to change the fact that I love you, you arrogant…" She petered out, clamping her mouth tightly shut.

"No." He closed his eyes for just a second. "You and I both know you can't possibly love me. You don't go from being engaged to one man to being in love with another in less than twenty-four hours." And certainly not him, not the real him in the light of day instead of some romanticized version she'd created based on last night.

She raised her chin defiantly. "Stranger things have happened. For some people it's love at first sight."

"I know." He'd taken one look at her and he'd known. But she hadn't taken one look at him and fallen in love with him. He'd simply cushioned the impact of Elliott's betrayal.

Some of her ire vanished. "Oh, God. I got so caught up… I'm sorry I threw myself at you. I forgot that you have someone."

He shook his head. "There is someone, but… Some of us were meant to be alone."

"No. I don't believe that. You're wonderful and tender and…I refuse to believe you were meant to be alone. If you really love her, go to her, Simon. Don't wait until it's too late."

Perfect case in point that she was still overwrought and emotionally unstable. "Make up your mind, Tawny. If you love me the way you say you do, why are you sending me to someone else?"

She gentled her hand against his cheek, her eyes shadowed with a sadness that lanced him. "Because I can't make you love me if you don't. And pride's just a thing. I'm not ashamed that I've fallen in love with you. I got exactly what I wished for. This is definitely a stiletto kind of love." She lowered her hand and offered a half-hearted smile. "This is hard, Simon. Tenacity's always gotten me a long way. I've managed to get almost everything I've ever wanted by cajoling or nagging. I know that about myself. But unfortunately I can't bulldog you into loving me. But that's why we're here. It's part of our purpose in life, to love and to be loved. So if you're in love with this woman, you've got to let her know. I'm not some psycho who wants you to be miserable and alone just because you don't want me. I want you to be happy."

She only thought she loved him. He knew it just wasn't possible. "Tawny, you're very special…."

She shook her head and held up a hand to stop him. "I don't think I can listen to you fill me in on my attributes. And before you go there, let me say I can't feel the way I do about you and be friends."

He shook his head. "No. I don't think we can be friends. It was a great night and you're a wonderful person, but you had it right last night when you said our paths were unlikely to cross again. You'll make some lucky guy very happy one day...."

She averted her face, wrapping her arms around herself as if she were cold, despite the sweltering heat. "I think it's time for you to leave."

Simon slung his camera case over his shoulder. "I'll drop the photos in the mail when I finish developing them. Give me a couple of days."

She walked to the door and threw the dead bolt. "Send me a bill with them."

"No. We discussed that up front. No bill."

"If you don't bill me, then I owe you a party. It'd be neater and tidier if you'd just invoice me." She raised her chin a notch, daring him to argue with her.

"I hope you find the man of your dreams, Tawny."

She looked him dead in the eye. "I did."

He walked out the door and closed it behind him. She was wrong. And one day she'd thank him for this.

TAWNY'S CELL PHONE RANG. For one heart-stopping moment she thought it might be Simon. She hoped he'd decided that last night was something special, that whatever it was between them was something special. Nope. Elliott's number flashed on the display.

"Hi, Elliott."

"Tawny, is Simon still there?"

"No. Try him on his cell," she said. Why hadn't he just called Simon in the first place? She didn't have time to play operator. She was too busy being miserable.

"I don't need to talk to him. I just wondered if he was there. I need to come over." Excitement tinged his voice. She wasn't up for any of Elliott's drama.

"I don't think so, Elliott. This is bad timing. I'm just not up to it."

"I've got something you need to see." He sounded practically aquiver.

She was too lethargic and generally miserable to argue with him. Elliott, the self-absorbed, probably wanted to show her a promise ring he'd designed for Richard or something equally inane. "Whatever. Come on over."

"Can I bring Richard?"

At least he'd asked permission. "Are the two of you joined at the hip now?"

Elliott laughed. "Naughty, naughty, Tawny."

Ugh. Poor choice of words. "Forget I said that. Come over whenever."

She kept herself busy tidying up her apartment and tidying herself up until Elliott arrived with Richard in tow. She might be rejected and dejected, but she didn't have to look like a hag or live like a slob.

Elliott and Richard arrived bearing iced Frappuccinos and half a dozen bagels with cream cheese and a side of lox from Abrusco's. Caffeine was good. Food was better.

She took the proffered food and placed it on the chest between the sofa and chair.

"Abrusco's was Richard's idea," Elliott said. Obviously he wanted her to like Richard. She wasn't sure she'd ever like him, but she'd aim for civility. "Thanks."

"There's a raisin-and-cinnamon with your name on it in there," Richard said.

"My favorite. Thanks again." She dug out the bagel and smothered it with fattening cream cheese. The better to blimp up with. She bit into it. Even a day old and unheated it was delicious.

"Don't you want to know what it is Richard and I have to show you?" Elliott asked, pulling out an onion bagel.

"Elliott, this better be really good because I'm just not much in the mood." Bagels or not.

"Let me guess." He smeared lox over an onion bagel—now Richard could endure onion-and-lox breath. "You told Simon how you felt, he rationalized everything for you and then he left."

"How'd you know? Did you talk to him?"

She'd rather have this conversation without Richard, but really it didn't matter. And he'd been quiet.

Not nearly as offensive this morning as he had been last night. Of course, she hadn't sniped at him either.

"I didn't have to talk to him. We've been friends for a long time." He gestured toward her with a plastic knife. "I told you you'd have to fight for him."

She felt empty inside. "I can't make him love me if he doesn't."

"If he loved you, would you fight for him?"

She winced. She'd known Elliott to be thoughtless often but never cruel. "If I thought he loved me, you know I'd fight."

Elliott smirked like the cat who'd just swallowed the canary. "I found out this morning Simon's kept a big secret from me."

"Yes?"

"I knew Simon was in love with someone, I just didn't know who. And he's not the kind of guy you press for details like that. And, well, I can be a little caught up in my own life, so I really hadn't pursued it very hard."

Was that a glimmer of self-awareness on his part? "You know, there is hope that you're not a total narcissist."

Richard sniggered but Elliott ignored her comment.

"I found out this morning just who Simon's mystery woman is."

Her heart shattered. Knowing Simon loved someone else was one thing. But really *knowing*…

"I thought you hadn't talked to him," she said.

"I haven't, darling. But a picture's worth a thousand words. Remember our engagement party at the gallery?"

"Of course I remember it. It was only two months ago and I planned it." Why did Elliott have to spin everything out? "Does everything have to be a drama with you? Can't you just get on with it? Who is she?"

"All in good time, Tawny. Indulge me for a moment. Richard took photos that night at our engagement party. We were looking back through them this morning."

Richard pulled a photo out of a padded envelope she hadn't noticed before and handed it to Elliott. Elliott passed it on to her. "What do you think?"

Simon, obviously unaware he was being captured on film, stared at someone off-camera. The stark longing etched on his face, the tenderness and pain in his eyes, felt like a knife to her heart. The expression on his face, in his eyes, was so private, so personal, she felt intrusive even looking. Richard had captured both the beauty and the sorrow of love. She looked away.

"I'd say that's the face of a man passionately in love," she said past the lump in her throat.

She felt sick. If that was at her engagement party, chances were she knew the woman he so deeply loved. Or perhaps not. Most of the guests had been Elliott's business acquaintances. It'd been a good opportunity for him to garner exposure for the gallery.

How could Elliott look so pleased when she felt like barfing?

"I agree," he said. "*That* was taken with a zoom lens. Richard took this one with the regular lens." He passed her another photo. "Take a look at the love of his life."

Tawny steeled herself to look down. The picture fluttered to the table, out of her nerveless fingers. Stunned, she stared at the photo of herself sitting alone at a table. Everyone had gotten up to dance and she'd needed a few minutes at the table alone. Simon sat one table over.

That yearning, that passion, was directed at *her*.

"But that's me," she whispered.

"Yeah. As I said, a picture's worth a thousand words. He loves you," Elliott said with a triumphant smirk.

Shock numbed her. "But it doesn't make any sense. This morning I told him how I felt, I told him I loved him, and he just walked away."

Elliott nodded. "He would."

"But why? I told him I loved him. He let me think he was in love with someone else and essentially told me to have a nice life."

"Ever since I've known him he's been emotionally neglected. Letitia and Charles aren't bad people and they're not cruel. And I think they've finally figured out what they did and want to make amends for it. They always had one another and Simon was left on his own. Thank God for his grandparents. If it hadn't been for them… But Simon's totally convinced he's unlovable."

She'd drawn similar conclusions from the little he'd told her about his childhood. But how could he possibly think himself unlovable? "Has he ever told you he's unlovable?"

"He doesn't have to. I'm falling back on clichés this morning, but if a picture's worth a thousand words, actions speak louder than words. He holds everyone at arm's length. I've been thinking a lot about Simon since we were at the hospital last night. I don't think he was always this way, although he was when I met him. I think when he was a kid, his parents just kept shutting him out and he finally decided it hurt less if he was the one who closed the door. His parents. Jillian, a girl from England. You. Even me sometimes."

It began to make a sad sort of sense. "Jillian married his cousin."

Elliott's eyebrows shot up. "You know about Jillian?"

"He mentioned her last night."

"I'm amazed."

"So, how did Jillian wind up married to his cousin?"

"She said once she got to know him, that he wasn't her cup of tea," Elliott said.

As suddenly as they'd gone out, without fanfare the lights blinked back on.

"Well, I guess I just shed some light on everything," Elliott drawled.

It was corny and Tawny rolled her eyes but laughed nonetheless. "Things are looking brighter by the minute."

"Oh. That was so bad. I think I'll excuse myself to your well-lit bathroom on that one."

Elliott stood and left the room.

Simon loved her. Her. Not some nameless, faceless, skinny paragon. He loved her! If she didn't understand his twisted logic, she might be tempted to pinch his head off for walking out on her this morning.

Already her apartment felt ten degrees cooler, which she knew was impossible. Perhaps it was that her heart felt so much lighter.

Richard cleared his throat and Tawny jumped. She'd forgotten all about him.

"I owe you an apology. It was wrong…. I was wrong…." He sighed. "This isn't coming out right. I'm not saying being gay is wrong. I can't believe loving someone is wrong. But for it to happen the way it did…while you were still engaged…I'm sorry for that. I'm sorry for any pain I've caused you. I don't expect you to be my friend, but for Elliott's sake, I don't want to be your enemy."

Tawny busied herself with walking around the room blowing out candles. She straightened from the last candle and looked at Richard. There was no animosity in his blue eyes, merely a guarded wariness. "I don't believe the end justifies the means, but better that Elliott discovered this now than after we were married." She paused and smoothed her fingers down the front of her shorts. "I'm not sure I can be your friend, but I'm not your enemy." She looked him square in the eye. "Unless you hurt Elliott—then all bets are off."

Richard blinked, obviously surprised. A smile crooked his mouth and he nodded. "Fair enough."

Elliott returned from the bathroom and looked from one to the other. "I feel as if I'm interrupting something."

"I'm just filling him in on all of your bad qualities, but I haven't had nearly enough time," Tawny said.

Elliott feigned amazement. "I was unaware I had any."

Tawny smiled angelically. "I could catch you up to speed if you had an hour or so."

"You're a sweetheart to offer, but I suspect you have better things to do with your time." Elliott picked up the photo of Simon and Tawny and studied it. "Here's the deal, Tawny. I think he's scared to trust that someone could actually love him. That it's not just a mistake. Simon knows all about how to love. He just doesn't know how to be loved."

She crossed her arms over her chest and smiled. "Well, he's about to learn."

He handed her the photo and grinned. "Feeling that way about you must scare the hell out of him.

And for you to tell him you loved him…I'm sure he's terrified." Elliott shook his head. "If I didn't know you're the best thing that could possibly happen to Simon, I'd feel sorry for the poor guy…almost."

13

"JUST A MINUTE!" SIMON yelled. Couldn't a guy find a moment of peace in his own apartment? First his father called on his cell phone after he'd dropped him off, then Elliott rang with some stuff and nonsense about staying home, now someone at the door.

He clattered down the grated stairs of his loft. At least the electricity was back on and he didn't have to worry about what would happen to Tawny after dark. If the electricity hadn't been restored by dusk, he'd planned to show up on her doorstep so she didn't have to endure the dark night alone. It would've been awkward, but he didn't want her alone and scared in the dark. Now that wouldn't be necessary.

Despite the return of power, and hence air-conditioning, it hadn't put a dent in the heat. He'd showered without shaving and thrown on running shorts and a T-shirt. He was clean, but he looked grungy. Grungy suited his mood.

He threw open the door and then wished he hadn't. Tawny stood on the other side. He stared at her. A sundress clung to her curves. Her hair was piled atop her head. Sunglasses hid her eyes. A back-pack purse was slung across her back.

"What are you doing here?" he asked. Rude and abrupt usually put people off.

"You might've had dismal parents, but I'm sure they taught you better manners than that. Aren't you going to ask me in?"

Of course, rude and abrupt didn't seem to work so well on Tawny.

"Come in." He ran his hand through his hair but stepped aside. He didn't feel particularly up to gracious, which wasn't his strong suit on a good day. And this wasn't a good day. "What are you doing here?" he repeated his earlier question. He left the door ajar as a not-too-subtle hint.

She closed the door and pushed her sunglasses to the top of her head. Her eyes sparkled. She looked positively radiant, and he was positively flummoxed.

"I'm here to collect on a promise."

She stepped closer, and the unique blend of perfume and Tawny triggered all those sensory things that made it bloody near impossible to think straight instead of thinking about having his face buried in her neck and his willy in her…. She *did not* need to come any closer.

"I didn't make any promises."

"It wasn't an exact promise. It was more along the lines of a promise of intent." She shrugged off her purse and held it in one hand. She looked him over from head to toe, sexual heat radiating from her, scorching him.

Simon shifted from one foot to the other, at a total loss. He'd walked out on her this morning and now she stood eyeing him as if he was a Popsicle on a summer day. And mother of God, he knew what she did with Popsicles. "Have you been drinking?"

Her slow smile simmered through him, heating him up. "Only a Frappuccino."

Focus, Simon. Not on her smile or Popsicles or the way her sundress hugged all of her curves. Focus on this conversation and getting her the hell out of this apartment before he did something really stupid like kiss her and beg her to stay. "What is this promise of intent?"

"You said if you had your lady love you'd know what to do with her." Another step brought her seriously into his personal space. Only a few inches of very hot air separated them. She smoothed her hand down his belly to the elastic band of his shorts, and his heart pounded like mad. "Well, I'm here, fully expecting to be—what was it?—oh, yes, fucked senseless for a week."

Bloody hell if that didn't catch Mr. Winky's attention. He had to get her out of here now. When she talked like that…

He sought to keep a cool head. Both of them. "What makes you think you're her?" She couldn't possibly know. He'd never breathed a word to anyone.

"Tell me I'm not." She pulled a photo out of her purse and held it out. Him, caught in a moment of weakness and utter misery, looking at her.

"Convince me this is a lie," she said.

He of all people knew the power of a photograph. How apropos. All these years he'd hidden behind his camera, only to be stripped naked, at his rawest in a photograph. He appreciated the irony.

He'd never convince her he didn't love her. But he knew she didn't really love him. She couldn't. He bracketed her shoulders with his hands and put her away from him. "Tawny, you're on the rebound. It's too soon. You don't really know me."

"Okay, I think you pulled out just about every argument you could. Now I'm going to debunk these myths you've created in that sexy head of yours. First, let's get it straight. Elliott wounded my pride." She stabbed at him with her finger. "You broke my heart. Second, it's too soon for what? Love doesn't come on a time line. It's not on-the-job training where you log in a certain number of hours for certification. And last, don't tell me I don't know you." She took her hand in his and brought it to her lips. "I knew you the second you climbed out on that ledge after my cat. I knew you when you held my hand in the dark. I knew you when you covered for Elliott. I knew you when you ran to your parents, literally, because they needed you, despite your history with them. I knew you when you dried me off and carried me to bed when I was too tired to move. There may be facets of you that I don't know yet, but don't tell me I don't know you."

It was one of the hardest things he'd ever done, because he really, really wanted to believe her. But he knew things she didn't. He knew that if she really knew him, knew that hollow core inside him, she couldn't possibly love him.

He pulled his hand away and put the width of the room between them. "Don't you understand?" He struggled to make her understand. "I'm like Hades. Lord of the Dark. You're Persephone. Light and beautiful. You don't belong with me."

Her mouth gaped open for a full five seconds. "Please tell me you don't actually believe any of that hogwash that just came out of your mouth."

Just when he thought he'd heard all of her Southernisms. "Did you just say 'hogwash'?"

"Don't you dare make fun of me and don't think you can distract me. How about this—do you actually believe the load of crap you just shoveled my way? That's just wrong. And why would I want to be that mealymouthed Persephone? If you're going to draw some crazy mythical analogies, at least make me some kick-ass goddess like Athena or Artemis. Not some ninny whose mama had to come rescue her." She tossed her backpack onto the sofa. "You know, I was going to call a therapist on Monday for myself. You should make an appointment instead."

"I do not need a therapist," he said. "And if I'm so wonderful, why are you already trying to change me?"

"I'm not trying to change you." She threw her hands up in the air. "I'm trying to get some positive self-awareness through that thick skull of yours. And you definitely need a therapist if you keep spouting that kind of crazy crap."

"You think it's crazy crap and that should totally invalidate my viewpoint?"

"Listen, buster, you're the one who told me I needed to pack up and move back home if I was going to let my parents' opinion run my life. You take your own advice and stop letting a set of lousy parents ruin your ability to have a relationship."

That hit remarkably close to home. "Why do you need a therapist?"

"Just so you don't think you're getting away with anything, I know you're deliberately changing the subject. You have a habit of doing that when the conversation isn't going your way. But I needed a therapist because you were driving me crazy."

Simon crossed his arms over his chest. Next she'd be commenting on his body language. She had nerve saying he drove her crazy. She made him loony. "How was I driving you crazy?"

"Well, not you personally, but you in those dreams. I couldn't figure out how I could love Elliott and be having those kinds of dreams about you every night. But now that's easy enough without a shrink." She put her hands on his shoulders. "I don't love Elliott. Well, except as something that's a cross between a brother and a friend. Not the way I love you."

She made it sound frightfully logical. "Oh."

"That's it? Oh? After all of that, the only thing you have to say to me is 'oh'?"

"What would you have me say?" He uncrossed his arms and dropped his hands to his sides.

She closed her eyes, as if her patience stood on its last leg, and delicately banged her head against his chest. "Simon, I believe we have a long, happy future ahead of us. I know in my heart that you love me. But it would be nice to hear it without me having to drag it out of you." She cupped his jaw in her hand. "I love you, Simon Thackeray. Now is it really so hard to put this—" she looked at the photo "— into words?"

The photo all but shouted it, but he said what she so obviously needed to hear.

"I love you." The stark beauty in those three simple words, and the accompanying vulnerability, shivered through him.

"Thank you." She looked so happy it nearly ripped him apart.

What if he didn't live up to her expectations? What if he simply didn't have it in him to be the man she thought he was? "But it doesn't really change anything."

"Like hell it doesn't change anything. You are

never getting rid of me, because I love you and I know you love me. Go ahead, retreat behind that wall of yours. If I have to go brick by brick and it takes me a lifetime, I'll tear it down. I'll crawl to hell and back if that's what it takes. All the other times I've been relentless and gone after what I wanted, that was just boot camp. This is the big event I've been training for. So be forewarned, this is war."

"You'll get tired. You'll figure it out, sooner rather than later, that I'm not this romanticized version you've painted in your head."

"You are so wrong. Please, never tell me I'm irrational. I'm not harboring any illusions. You're arrogant and opinionated and sarcastic and really sort of bossy."

"You just called me bossy?"

"That's why we're so perfect together. You don't intimidate me because I'll hand it right back to you." She sat on the sofa and pulled him down beside her. "You told me that you were scared when you went out on that ledge. It's okay to be frightened. That's what bravery and courage are all about. It doesn't require courage to face what you don't fear. It's okay to be frightened, but it's not okay to run away from it."

Hadn't Elliott told him, in the early morning hours at the hospital, that Simon feared being happy? Maybe he'd been onto something.

"You don't seem to fear anything except the dark." Even as he said it he realized that though she feared the dark, she'd gone down those seven flights of pitch-black stairs with him, for him.

"That's not true. I'm scared to death I won't get through to you. I'm so scared of losing you I'm shaking inside." She held up her hand and he could see that it was, indeed, less than steady.

"And you really think that would be such a bad thing?"

"Infinitely worse than being trapped in the dark alone. Where else am I going to find someone to worship and adore this ass?" She flashed him a cheeky grin and then sobered. She held her hand out to him, palm up. "I'm standing here emotionally naked, Simon. Climb out on this ledge with me."

She was wearing him down, making him believe. There really was something akin to magic about her, because he found himself believing. Teetering on the brink of being convinced that she just might love him, warts and all. She'd gone into the dark with him, only needing him to hold her hand. And now she offered the same in return. He felt the dark emptiness inside him, that always seemed to hover at the periphery of his soul, slip away.

He placed his hand in hers and brought their clasped hands to his mouth, pressing a kiss to her hand. "You really do love me, don't you?" He didn't attempt to mask the wonderment in his voice.

She smiled as if he'd handed her the moon, and he was humbled that he had the capability to do so.

"Hello. That's what I've been saying. You know, you have an attention problem."

He eased onto the sofa and she scooted onto his lap and wrapped her arms around his neck. Simon clasped her head in his hand.

"I love you," he said and kissed her, a tender promise. "I love you," he said again. It had a nice ring and it didn't sound nearly as frightening as he'd anticipated. He kissed her again, liking the pattern he had going. Except this time he kissed her longer, harder, deeper, mating his tongue with hers.

They came up for air and she wiggled her delightful bottom against his erection. She had him hot and hard with just a kiss. And before he totally abandoned himself to pleasure, he wanted an answer to something that had earlier seemed unimportant.

"Luv, I've got a question."

"Just for the record, I like that *luv* business. It makes me hot. Now ask away."

"Where did you get the photograph?"

"Elliott gave it to me." She nuzzled his neck. "You should check out my undies, I think you'll find them…interesting."

He slid his hand beneath her dress— "Elliott took that photo?"—past her thighs, anticipating a thong or sexy lace. Instead his fingers encountered hot, slick flesh surrounded by lace. Heat surged through him. "Oh, luv, these are *very* interesting." He traced the outline of her wet lips, bared by the lacy opening, with one finger.

"Crotchless. I came armed for heavy-duty battle." She smiled and teased the tip of her tongue against her lower lip. "It's Richard's picture."

He tugged her dress up past her thighs, exposing a pair of black crotchless panties and her wet folds. "So Elliott ratted me out."

She laughed and spread her legs. "Yes. It was Elliott."

Simon slid a finger into her silky channel and she moaned deep in her throat, turning him on even more.

"I love it when you make those sounds. It makes my cock hard."

"And I love it when you talk like that and touch me that way. It makes me wet. But you know that firsthand."

Yes. He knew that intimately, arousingly. "Remind me to thank Elliott later. Much later. Next week perhaps. Right now I've got a promise to keep."

Epilogue

A *year later*

"NERVOUS?" SIMON ASKED, taking her hand in his.

Tawny looked out from their vantage point in Elliott's office at the guests milling about the gallery. Everything was in place. Music. Caterer. Guests.

"A little. I've never planned a wedding before. Even an unofficial one. Why? Are you nervous?"

He rimmed his finger beneath the neck of his tuxedo shirt. "I'm not so fond of the bloody monkey suit and I'd prefer not to stand in front of a crowd, but overall I'm fine."

She eyed him from head to toe, flirting with him. "You clean up very nicely." And that was a gross understatement. He was mouth-wateringly yummy in the formal black tie and tails. "I might have to get you into a tux more often."

His look sizzled over her, setting her hormones into a frenzy. Of course, with Simon it didn't take much to stir her up. "I'd rather you concentrate on getting me *out* of the tux."

"That can be arranged later. Do you think your parents will come?" she asked.

Simon shrugged with studied nonchalance. "I expect they might."

He still tensed, still had a stiffness about him whenever Letitia or Charles was mentioned. But he and they had made progress, albeit baby steps, in the last year.

"I think they genuinely regret your train wreck of a childhood. At least they're trying."

"I'm trying, as well. Do you really think people can change?"

"You know the answer to that. The only thing that limits us is fear and the boundaries we set for ourselves."

"Our relationship has helped me understand them better." He brushed his hand along her jaw. "I think Mum and Dad have a relationship similar to ours. Even after thirty years he's still head over heels in love with her."

Finally, after a year, he was beginning to believe, truly believe, in his heart and in his gut that she loved him. That she wasn't going to wake up and decide there just wasn't enough substance to him or that the substance was too unpalatable.

He'd actually gone to Savannah with her a couple of months ago to meet her family, after the fallout from her broken engagement had cleared. It'd been an interesting weekend. While Elliott, with his outgoing personality, had charmed them, they'd actually liked Simon better—especially after they'd found out Elliott's sexual preference. Her father had pronounced Simon a man of depth. Her sister Betsy just thought he was weird, but then again, anyone not teeing off at the golf course or signing on at the garden club was weird to her sister, who lived in a microcosmic world.

And she knew for sure Simon was getting comfortable with their relationship when he asked her to go with him to England in the fall to meet his grandparents. Who knew? In a decade or so, her relationship-phobic love might actually decide to do something wild and crazy, like commit.

"Speaking of being head over heels…where is the happy couple of the day?" she asked.

Simon grinned. "Richard was nervous, so Elliott thought it best if they had a few minutes alone before the ceremony." He tugged again at his tie. "A gay commitment ceremony held in an art gallery—not exactly conventional. You'd think they would've picked something a little more avant garde than a tux."

"Would you like a little cheese with that whine? Anyway, Richard wanted tuxedos and Elliott wanted to make sure everything was the way Richard wanted it. I think it's sweet. Richard's been good for Elliott."

"Absolutely. He's much more considerate than he ever was before."

"And I think it's very cool they chose the anniversary of the blackout."

"Very sentimental. Very touching."

She shoved his shoulder. "Don't be a jerk." She knew better than anyone what a sentimental romantic he was at heart.

"But I'm so good at it." He smirked, sending her heart into a flutter and a heat blooming low in her belly.

"You're good at lots of things," she said and smirked back.

"Stop it. It won't do for you to go tenting the front of my trousers with naughty insinuations before the ceremony."

"You know how to spoil a girl's fun."

"I'll make it up to you later, luv." And he would…and then some. "You know what today is, don't you? We've been together a year and we've got some unfinished business between us we need to wrap up."

"Business?" What was he talking about? And his timing left a lot to be desired.

"Right. I delivered your photographs, but you've yet to plan my party."

"You were supposed to bill me," she said, her mind wandering to her mental checklist. Had the caterer ordered the extra champagne Elliott had requested? Yikes! She thought they'd answered her e-mail, but she didn't recall seeing the extra bottles.

"Now don't do getting all argumentative, luv. I need an event planned."

Men picked the weirdest times. She focused her attention on him. "What kind of event?" Simon wasn't a party kind of guy. He could've been voted Least Likely to Attend a Party in his high school yearbook.

"Something very similar to this. Except perhaps a bit fancier. Maybe something in a church and then a party afterward with a bit of dancing."

Was he saying what she thought he was saying? Her heart seemed to skip a beat. Perhaps he had impeccable timing after all. "Are you talking about a wedding and a reception?"

He snapped his fingers. "That's it."

"You're definitely sure? It's a lot of work if you think you might change your mind later."

"I've never been more certain of anything in my life."

"I presume you have someone in mind?"

"As a matter of fact, there's this enchanting creature who has me thoroughly besotted…."

"And have you asked her yet?"

"I'm working on it." He took her hand in his and dropped to one knee. "Tawny Marianne Edwards, would you marry me?"

She'd always thought it was sort of goofy when guys got on one knee in the movies. It wasn't. It was sweet and tender, and if he made her cry and her mascara ran she'd kill him. "I would love to do just that, Simon Trevor Thackeray."

He reached into his pocket and pulled out a velvet ring box. "I'd be honored if you'd wear my ring."

Oh my. He was doing this right. He opened it and pulled out an exquisite pear-cut diamond ring that was large…make that really large…forget it, they were talking *bling*.

"Do you like it?" he asked.

"No. I love it." He slipped it onto her finger. "It's beautiful." She waffled her hand back and forth, catching the light in the myriad facets of the stone. Call her tacky, crass, shallow and/or materialistic, but she'd always wanted a big ring, and her man had delivered. "It's a rock."

"It's as big as your sister's?"

She grinned at him. "Yeah. This'll blind her."

"And it's bigger than Elliott's?"

She presumed they were still talking about the ring. "Definitely bigger than Elliott's. It must have cost a fortune."

He slid his arms around her and pressed a sweet kiss to her temple. "You're worth it, luv. And anyway, it was easy money. I sold some of those photos of you in the bath to an Internet porn site."

She grinned at his wicked, warped sense of humor and slid her arms about his neck.

The unmistakable click of a camera sounded. She and Simon both glanced toward the sound just as Richard fired off another shot.

"Now that I've caught the happy ending on film,

do you think we could get on with this wedding?"
Richard asked with a nervous smile.

Tawny laughed and didn't correct him. This
wasn't a happy ending…this was just the beginning.

If you enjoyed what you just read,
then we've got an offer you can't resist!

Take 2 bestselling love stories FREE!

Plus get a FREE surprise gift!

Clip this page and mail it to Harlequin Reader Service®

IN U.S.A.	IN CANADA
3010 Walden Ave.	P.O. Box 609
P.O. Box 1867	Fort Erie, Ontario
Buffalo, N.Y. 14240-1867	L2A 5X3

YES! Please send me 2 free Harlequin® Blaze™ novels and my free surprise gift. After receiving them, if I don't wish to receive anymore, I can return the shipping statement marked cancel. If I don't cancel, I will receive 6 brand-new novels each month, before they're available in stores! In the U.S.A., bill me at the bargain price of $3.99 plus 25¢ shipping and handling per book and applicable sales tax, if any*. In Canada, bill me at the bargain price of $4.47 plus 25¢ shipping and handling per book and applicable taxes**. That's the complete price and a savings of at least 10% off the cover prices—what a great deal! I understand that accepting the 2 free books and gift places me under no obligation ever to buy any books. I can always return a shipment and cancel at any time. Even if I never buy another book from Harlequin, the 2 free books and gift are mine to keep forever.

151 HDN D7ZZ
351 HDN D72D

Name	(PLEASE PRINT)	
Address	Apt.#	
City	State/Prov.	Zip/Postal Code

Not valid to current Harlequin® Blaze™ subscribers.

Want to try two free books from another series?
Call 1-800-873-8635 or visit www.morefreebooks.com.

* Terms and prices subject to change without notice. Sales tax applicable in N.Y.
** Canadian residents will be charged applicable provincial taxes and GST.
   All orders subject to approval. Offer limited to one per household.
® and ™ are registered trademarks owned and used by the trademark owner and/or its licensee.

BLZ05   ©2005 Harlequin Enterprises Limited.

MORE BLACKOUT TIPS

*When the lights go out,
absolutely anything
is possible....*

6. Put on your poker face.

You've always wanted to learn, he's always promised to teach you. Now is the time! For an added adventure, there is always strip poker.

7. Get plenty of exercise.

Go running together after dinner in the dark—right down the center of the road. Don't say a word to each other, just work up a good sweat.

8. So, he can't watch the game on TV before bed...

Grab a candle and read Blaze out loud.

9. Let me count the ways...

Remember mail? Actual mail, not e-mail or text messages? Write secret love notes to him and hide them in unexpected spots around the house. Sooner or later he'll thank you....

10. High school reunion?

Get in your car, put the high beams on and drive to that perfect spot to look at the stars. It might not be called Lookout Point anymore, but it's never too late to find out exactly what's involved in "heavy petting."